Alan Fraser is an international development consultant, at present, working in Kenya. He was with the UN in New York for eight years and maintains a home in Westchester County for his estranged family. He is domiciled in Scotland.

Born in the British military sector of Berlin, he spent his formative years in West Germany. After his German mother left him, he grew up in Edinburgh. He ran away from his domineering father, joining the army as a private. He fought his way to university, married and had four children.

Perfection

ALAN FRASER

Perfection

Chimera

CHIMERA PAPERBACK

© Copyright 2016
Alan Fraser

A CIP catalogue record for this title is
available from the British Library.

ISBN 978 1903136 54 6

Chimera is an imprint of
Pegasus Elliot MacKenzie Publishers Ltd.
www.pegasuspublishers.com

First Published in 2016

Chimera
Sheraton House Castle Park
Cambridge England

Printed & Bound in Great Britain

Death is simply another form of life,
but experienced in a different place.

Preamble

Have you ever had the pleasure of flying to Sierra Leone and specifically, Freetown? At least when you fly into Bhutan's Thimphu, there is ground all around; searing mountains certainly, as you bank steeply to land and indeed, even more frightening when taking off. The airport at Addis Ababa is actually in the town; a stone's throw from Bole Road; the centre of much in that town. Freetown however is something else. The airport is on an island. At low tide, it is possible to drive there but it's a long drive. The cheapest and most tortuous way to cross to Freetown, at least one hour away, is by ferry; a large car-carrying monster of a vessel. The next option is by hydrofoil – when it works. One time, the engine conked out just as it approached the landing area. Unfortunately, it was carrying some British local government politicians. They had to wade – though no deeper than waist height – to dry land. The quickest, if you could afford it or if you were a UN employee, is by helicopter, a ten minute ride away. The UN's flying machine was particularly entertaining. Not only were you carried by Russian (but probably Soviet-era) helicopters but also the pilots (always two) were burly and Russian; every inch Russian spy material, for a novel or even a film.

As John flew both ways every month or so, he would almost swoon at the sight of the Bintumani Hotel, a Chinese owned and managed establishment. It had three attractions: a swimming pool (when the water wasn't green), stunning views out to sea and a promontory location that captured the breeze. This was particularly welcomed when the heat was intense and the humidity overpowering.

For John, it also had a few suites to rent at a reasonable rate. The beds were pristine clean and the duvets white and light. The food was a bit challenging – all that Chinese cuisine – but he got by. The suite – in truth, a small studio apartment – was ideal for his routine of working, eating and sleeping. Sometimes other aspects of life featured. This is the story of one such…

1.

They sat in the open terrace of his apartment's restaurant. John was hosting Lorraine and Kate. Lorraine was discovered on craigslist after his disappointment elsewhere. Quite simply, he was 'cruising' but not in the old fashioned way of driving along seedy thoroughfares at night, looking for some 'company'. This was the electronic version and after a couple of false starts, all seemed 'set fare'. Lorraine was tall, slender and seductive. The apartment manager referred to her as "hot", she having been introduced to the front office staff as a future regular visitor. The Chinese staff seemed to have no qualms about such an arrangement.

Kate was slighter and with an engaging smile. The occasion was simply for John to be introduced to a friend of Lorraine, Kate being a business – Lorraine referred to it as her 'enterprise' – partner. The meal went well, a bottle of wine was quaffed and once finished, they went to his apartment. They wanted to talk about the business idea and John's business acumen could be useful.

He offered another bottle of wine. It made all feel warm, glowing even. They were now settled on the settee: John to the right, then Lorraine and finally, Kate. John noticed them inching closer as they talked of nothing in particular. Hands were being clasped, whispers exchanged. John just sipped his wine quietly and watched.

Suddenly, they were kissing; not just a gentle peck on the cheek but an almost immediate passion. Their tongues flashed in the light, entwining like snakes' heads, fighting for the dominant position. John looked askance, wondering what to do. This was not planned.

He was sucked into the fray, kissing Lorraine, then Kate. The feel and taste of forbidden fruit took hold. It was already electrifying.

The girls – the women of course – were now groping at each other's clothes. John became a key instrument. He was almost attacking Kate's jeans. They were skin tight but were pulled – actually yanked – off successfully. Lorraine had already dispensed with hers; she was naked and panting. She kissed John and. in so doing, acknowledged both his role and, indeed, his skilful acquiescence. He was to start on Kate, Lorraine's face confirming as such. He wasn't convinced. He set an innocent trap.

Kate was now naked. She was sprawling. John put one hand on each thigh and pushed them apart. Her cunt was already glistening with pre-cum. He took Lorraine, almost forcibly by her head and encouraged her down to Kate's secret place.

"Lick her! Drink her! Drive her crazy!"

There was no hesitation, she dived in, with slurps audible as the licking and tongue penetration proceeded. By now, John was naked too, his erection strong and therefore plain for both to see. He kissed Kate on her mouth. She darted her tongue into his mouth as he was trying the same to her. She was intense.

Lorraine emerged, her mouth engorged. John kissed it, kissed her and tasted Kate's secretions lingering on Lorraine's delicious lips.

"Fuck her, John. I want you to fuck her. I want to watch!"

"I need to fuck you first, baby!"

She would have none of it and by then had already produced a condom. She put it on for him and steered his manhood to Kate's beckoning cunt. His cock-head was placed skilfully.

"Fuck her, John! I want you to fuck her and fuck her hard! I mean it! She wants it. I know she wants it."

With such entreaties, how could he resist? He started, slowly at first, then harder and harder still. No sooner had he started, she was almost screaming with pleasure. John looked at Lorraine. She smiled and kissed him. He withdrew, pulled off the sheath and plunged straight into Lorraine. He pumped and pumped then slowed down. Her occasional technique was to masturbate while he was lodged inside her. She did and Kate thrilled at the sight of it. Lorraine's self-induced and John's assisted pleasure came with deep satisfaction, a warm kiss and a lingering smile.

"Fuck her again, John! She needs it and I want to see it!"

"My god, Lorraine! Are you crazy?"

"Fuck me, John!" Kate called out. "She wants to see you again, fucking me like the cunt I am!"

He needed no second invitation, just another condom. Lorraine's timing was impeccable, tearing the packet, opening and peeling it on to John's still pulsating manhood. He was fucking her hard again and, within a minute or so, she exploded once more... He looked to Lorraine for reassurance. Smiles and kisses followed. He withdrew and let Kate recover. He went down on Lorraine and took his fill of her; there was lots of it. It was delicious. With the condom off, he entered Lorraine. She fought him as if to push him off. He was confused but as she did so, he achieved a rare climax; spoilt as she managed to extricate herself just as the magic moment struck. He looked at her askance and genuine confusion. There was no apparent reason that he could discern anyway.

In a sort of perverse retribution, Lorraine was now encouraged to lie down with her legs open. John wanted to see Kate reciprocating Lorraine's tongue gymnastics on Lorraine. She did. She lingered. Lorraine moved gracefully, her pelvic muscles signalling her response. John was now kissing Lorraine's mouth deeply. She came.

Things quietened down a bit as they took some more wine. Kate turned to Lorraine. "Can John fuck me again?"

Lorraine agreed. She saw John climb on to her – now lying, in Ancient Roman fashion, on the settee – and, before he knew it, he had slipped into her without a condom...

***

The atmosphere became sullen. Lorraine now drank copiously, smoked heavily, insisted that John buy a big bottle of Jamieson whiskey – the Irish version – and proceeded to become helpless in her drinking and smoking binge. Kate tried to talk to her but there was little response. Kate and John looked at each other and wondered what was going on.

It was now late anyway. John cleared up a little and all three found their way into the bedroom. Lorraine lay on her left shoulder. Kate moved into position, caressing Lorraine's back. John came last, tentatively close to Kate but still trying to communicate with Lorraine, with no luck.

Kate then asked Lorraine. "Will you let John fuck me again?"

"Do what you want!" was the curt reply.

There was no encouragement in the voice, only the implied threat of trouble ahead if he did. He left the bed and the room, closed the door quietly behind him, lay on the settee and tried to sleep. He wondered if one or both would have pity on him, eventually, summon him back to bed and sandwich him between them. There was nothing and this was *his* apartment!

***

Sunday morning revealed the flat tidied up, the 'do not disturb sign' still on the door. The two gorgeous women, who had fucked and been fucked, emerged. Kate was fine. Lorraine was anything but. She started smoking and drinking again. While Kate telephoned the chaperone of her two young children, John went into the bedroom. Lorraine followed.

"I saw you! I fucking saw you, falling in love with her!"

John was dumbfounded. "It's you I love!"

"You've taken her number! You've taken her e-mail address!"

He had done neither.

"Why don't you date her?"

At that moment, he thought she was relenting; moving back into the delightfully dark side of things.

"If that's what you want, why not? But you're part of it."

It was the wrong answer. It reinforced what he later discovered to be her perpetual illusion of betrayal.

"How could you fuck her without a condom? How could you…"

Before the sentence was finished, he blurted out to her, "It was an accident!"

It *was* an accident.

They both re-emerged. Kate was now trying to placate Lorraine further. She started shouting obscenities at him. John was in disbelief. Kate kept trying to calm her down. John knew that if and when Kate left, things would become uncomfortable. Twenty minutes later Kate was gone. John was now alone with a semi-drunk (again already and this was before noon) and verbally vicious woman. All he could think of was ways to get her to leave as well.

***

He started trying to talk to Lorraine, to show her affection. Things quietened down, then erupted, quietened down, then erupted again. She was now binge drinking and chain smoking. It was hideous.

More accusations came.

John heard a drawer opening and the clink of cutlery. Fuck! She was threatening to harm herself, cutting at her wrist. John had to wrench the knife from her! It was momentarily violent. Things quietened down as she started looking at old clips from American Idol. It seemed to bring calm to the mind.

Then eruption again.

"You've taken Kate's number. I know you have! I know it!" and with that, she tried to open his phone. That was anathema to him. What was in his phone was none of her business. It was another violent seizure. She screamed. A few minutes later, there was a knock at the door. It was the hotel's security officer, an uncharacteristically large Chinese gentleman. He asked if everything was OK. She appeared, feigned normality and John breathed with relief.

She went to bed and fell asleep. He checked if she was sound. She was.

He went downstairs and talked to the trusted senior receptionist. He suggested that he would try and wake her up so that she could leave at six p.m. He came back, looked in on her again; she was still sleeping.

The moment came, he started to try and wake her. The reaction was verbally awful, a chain of expletives. 'Management' turned up, tried to persuade her to dress and leave but she refused point blank! He asked 'management' to leave, conceding that he had agreed to let her stay.

She was now furious, demented even. He ordered food for her. She ate sort of, talked sort of, settled down and watched TV. John couldn't believe it. This was by far and away the worst day of his adult life. It was disgusting in the worst possible sense.

Tiredness finally took its toll. She went to bed and in order to ensure nothing untoward happen, he joined her. She did not object. She had already called her trusted cab driver to collect her at seven a.m. They lay together in 'spoons'. They fell asleep.

*****

It must have been the middle of the night. There was movement. John woke to find himself with a stonking erection. Given what had passed between them the previous eighteen hours, this was nothing short of extraordinary. He manoeuvred into a rear-entry position. She moaned and responded, again and again, with increasing enthusiasm. It became more and more passionate. Words of love started appearing; he languished in the extremes of verbal lust. She came. They finished. At six thirty a.m., the alarm went. They were both groggy. To her credit, she managed to get up, put clothes on and gathered her things to leave.

"I can't go through reception!"

He understood: it would be embarrassing for him too. He sneaked her out the back entrance, steadying her on his arm. She climbed into the taxi, the gates opened and she was gone.

"I'll never see that woman again," he swore to himself.

*****

That night, he felt genuine fear that she would arrange for two men to come and beat him up. This was not unheard of for a woman who perceived herself to being 'wronged'! The African dimension added a little more credence to the possibility. He focused his mind on packing; he was leaving in two days for Christmas in the UK and the US with his estranged family. Brussels Airlines would carry him to that city, then on to New York.

The following morning, he expressed his fears to 'management'. They assured him of their protection; the local security service and, if necessary, the police. He remained slightly unconvinced. The following day, it was time to leave.

With his packing complete and his eleven thirty p.m. flight all set, he decided not to wait all day in his apartment, just in case...

His driver came at one p.m. They drove into Freetown and had a meal and a beer. He went on to his favourite massage parlour, a genuine service for genuine release of body tension. Their conversation used up some time. By three thirty p.m., they were at the heliport. He wondered if two burly men would be standing near the entrance. He moved swiftly, showed his passport and boarding pass (printed earlier) and walked in. He still didn't feel safe. The Russians started the engine, the craft shuddered then lifted off the ground. As it manoeuvred, it swivelled to reveal the delightfully odd-shaped hotel with its hexagonal pool – now with pristine clear water. The open sea beckoned.

Ten minutes later, he saw passport control, a welcome sight.

"Which flight?"

"Brussels Airlines."

"You have a long wait."

"I just want to savour the prospect of flying home." Which was true, sort of. What he really wanted to savour was his escape.

Eight hours later, he was boarding the plane; he was first. An hour thereafter, the engines were roaring as it came off the tarmac and plunged into the dark night sky.

***

He did not want to open his e-mail account. Eventually, he had to, but this time in the comfort of his workroom; he never called it his study, which was a little too pretentious for his liking. In any case, since the break-up of the marriage, he had declined to sleep in the marriage bed and room. His workroom, with all his academic books around, was also where he slept. He felt cosy and safe in that room. He recognised an addressee he did not want to see. He opened, nervously…

Hello John!

In bed, clean and warm, starting to watch the series The Affair.

I just talked to Kate. She told me she gave you her email?

Please my love, don't hurt me.

I love you.

This was not so but then he discovered the unbalanced minds of all concerned. Then another message came.

Dear John,
Don't worry, I will not be a problem in your life again, I wish you the best, a better woman and a better life.
I am sorry for everything that transpired, from the bottom of my heart. I should not have introduced you to my friend; biggest mistake that I ever made but regrets are not important.
Safe travels; enjoy your family.
Don't reply as it's not necessary.
All the best.

'Dear Lorraine,

Just to say how much I appreciate this note from you; thank you! Got home twenty minutes ago to a cold, windswept, grey and wet England.

Take care,

John.

***

The entire episode had started so well (the initial fucking of Kate in front of Lorraine, at her request, was delicious). It descended into an absolute hell; again, by far and away, the worst night and following day and yet another night, in his entire adult life. There was certainly excessive suspicion on her part. It may even have amounted to paranoia but he was no psychologist. He was certainly a student of the human condition – the erotic side of life – but that did not qualify, yet her suspicions were extreme.

Then came the passive and conciliatory messages; a calm 'signing off' – a stark contrast to her verbal vitriol, bordering on self-harm and latent violence. The 'sign-off' was much to his relief. He could think of nothing more pleasing than to be released from the prospect of (even occasional) binge-drinking and excessive smoking, neither of which John was ever involved with in his life.

The sex had been terrific for the brief time he had known her – one tempestuous month – but that was not going to compensate for the anguish she had caused him. Indeed, if he had caused her the same, they were both best rid of each other.

2.

One day later.

John,
I am going to break a promise to myself and write this letter, I hope you read and understand where I come from with the horrendous stuff that happened over the last few days.

Like I told you before, the last time I had this unreasonable explosive behavior was when I had my first threesome with my ex; it was terrible. It was with another friend. He did exactly what you did (my / our fault, as we had not established the rules first). There was a point when I felt like you were giving her more attention than me. That point is when I started boiling with rage. I must have tried to block it with alcohol (because I remember the first good time). I have this misconception in my stupid head, that if I am in a relationship with a person that I love with my whole being and him, I would feel some kind of partnership when we are in the midst of it. I am always proved wrong. So, instead of accepting that that's how the world works, instead I react like a buffoon.

It has been an accumulation of my little hurts. Since I met you, your phone has always been off when I am around (would you believe that I have never cared about that before?). The condoms after that little previous tiff, the 'Cal ad' that you replied to a few hours after another tiff. Lord! I am definitely not an angel, John. My faults are there and I hate and resent myself for letting you see my insecurities in such an ugly manner and for that I apologise profusely.

I craved and still do for understanding and respect in an open and fulfilling relationship. I should know better as I have been here before. Everything that I said about me finding men to fuck me was just a furious outlet because it made sense to me at that angry moment, I really wanted to hurt you as much as you had hurt me. Everyone who knows me knows that I am always at home and would not give a toss about men living in Sierra Leone, visitors or residents. My head would not allow me to fuck around like so many people are so happy to do in this country. People make fun of me all the time. So you were never in danger of experiencing that.

The police? Are you kidding me? What would I do or report to them about you? Calling all my *friends? I did not even have credit. That was a drunken, childish rage, a helpless rage working. When you told me that you were ready to date my friend, at the flick of a finger… I felt… still do feel, like the most stupid woman in the world. I was ready for you. That's why I finally, reluctantly but fully, opened my cobwebbed soul, I have not been in love in such a long time. I don't remember ever feeling like this for a long time. It was a surprise, a very scary surprise. Wow!*

I am sorry, Mr. John. I had to write this letter before you leave. I wish I could make peace but I guess it's too late.

I sincerely wish you the best in all your endeavors. Please take care of your beautiful self. Be careful when having intercourse. Follow your dreams. Don't give up on your writing. You are really GREAT as I am sure you have been told by many.

I will concentrate more on my work now and hopefully this pain and missing you will ease up a bit, if ever.

Yours almost FOREVER.

It was never his intention to be in contact with this beautiful fucking and ugly beast of a woman but he found himself relenting.

This was a very courageous thing to write!

My causing you such pain was never intended and will remain an accident on so many levels.

You are correct though about 'ground rules'.

Let me tell you something, though. I have never (and I mean NEVER) been complimented by a person so many times and on various aspects of my appearance, performance, bearing and so much more; things like acknowledging that I walk straight upright, and so on.

As for my libido: yes, my former partner (we broke up five years ago) mentioned it a few times but you – you praised me so often.

I'm going to finish by citing part of a book review I wrote on Amazon, under my pen-name.

'P.S. For (me), the author and reviewer, page 240 perhaps carries his epitaph: *'people who deeply love each other cannot always live together; this is the real sadness of life'*.

I wish you all the best and so much more.

John,

So glad you got home safely and thank you for your positive reply.

I would give anything to have that getaway time away on my own, especially after such an exciting and, at the same time, horrible weekend. I hope you get good rest, healing reflecting time and a fabulous time with your beautiful family.

I have been working my ass off the whole of today without rest with the most horrible period cramps, with you constantly in my thoughts; not an easy feat. You know what happened today, when I had the courage to look back at our short history? Maybe I am wrong here. Kenema was dramatic to say the least. I have done the same dramatic stuff (maybe over the top), breaking and making up, exact things that happened in our brief and oh so recent past. I know that because I read your book after Kenema.

It's dawning on me that all my negative reactions to even a suspicion of being cheated on still makes me sick. I have to deal with that as it's my own journey and should not involve anyone else. It's not like I don't know all this as a principle; a principle that has steered me away from arguments and pettiness for a very long time. I cannot explain how I would let this happen in the first place, yet you are the first man that I can confidently say that I truly cared how you felt. I watched your every move after some time (because I am guarded) and I was sure, with every fibre of my body, that I was in love, finally, with a man that I admired, found hot and who complimented my crazy hidden desires. I was finally open to other, yet to be found, fantasies. That has been my dream for a long time. Yet when I finally had YOU, my ULTIMATE desire coming true, I found it hard to open up. I cannot explain why. I know you wondered. I got scared early on then you realized and I guess I have unconsciously been fighting against it until the opportunity came (last Saturday) and it just had to come out in the most horrible way.

I would so much want to be with you, in an adult kind of relationship but if I traumatized you too much, I understand if you wouldn't want to be with me.

I wish you the best too, and more.

As I walk through the hallways of my mind, I want to cling to the good memories; how you would look at me with such hunger that it made me blush and feel warm; your beautiful self, naked with only an apron on, serving me chilli...

I would like to show you how much that is not me! Has never been me! That was ugly.

I love you. Are you telling me that if I fuck up (at whatever degree), that I am fucked up forever? If so (safe for you) tell me. I cannot eat, drink, think, function. This new reality has truly messed me.

So sorry. I envy you. Maybe with a fireplace at your place, coffee? (Should be tea.) At least forgive me?

So sorry... when I am sad, inebriated and somehow unsettled, I cannot let it go; you especially. Do you hate me? Why?

He replied.

I certainly don't hate you but I caused the worst and most frightening day in my adult life.

I am damn sorry, I know when I am in love, in my desperate state, I do not really know and how and why I feel this way... haven't we been here before? You understand the pain and anxiety and really, you would rather just I go through it? I have not slept for three days. I am losing it. I guess, you do not care?

I care about your pain because I helped to uncover it - with unthinking actions but never on purpose. PLEASE let us just move into peace and wish each other well.

3.

John,

I care too that you had to see the unsightly sight. That is NOT me. I don't like that person and WILL not be her. Thank you for accepting my apologies.

Don't blame yourself for anything that happened. It was mixture of a two-day binge that was mixed with an almost manic euphoria. I hate myself terribly for losing control. Truly, I am sorry.

I finally found my mate, I like and loved every bit of time that we had together. I just realise now (I still can't sleep), that I was taking it for granted and we have loved, broken up, almost hated each and yet get back to each other because we are a fit. I was in the security that you would understand me at all times, which is ridiculous. Then I behaved like a little brat that didn't get her way. I don't think my body would want the touch from another man; I couldn't even fathom it in my head. I know everyone says that, but I know! I found you! If anything, this would be the ultimate test, to even sign and see where our loyalties, love and doubts are. Don't you owe me at least that, I want to show me to you as the loving, caring me; no game me. I want you to know ME.

We can get over this, I promise.

I want to pick you up from the airport; say yes. Oh, John!

I just read that end of your book (which book?).

I hope you don't mean that we have more in common than not.

He replied curtly:

You are not to pick me up from the airport. You are not to take me to Bintumani.

***

Let's try to know each other newly... through mail.

We can't forget what transpired but we can use this time apart, writing long e-mails. Ask anything and everything. Let's know each other anew. Maybe that was the problem in the first place? Too much, too soon including falling in love, jumping through or by-passing 'getting to

know each other'. If we start again, it will be a
lot of fun. Can you imagine?
Please say 'yes'?

I REALLY DON'T KNOW. I really don't. I am, however, going to write you, one rule-making message. You'll understand when you read it; maybe on Sunday.

Harking back to that awful night and following day. You would have cut yourself if I hadn't grabbed you forcibly. You would have scanned my phone if I hadn't barged to rescue it. What the fuck business is my phone to you anyway? I cannot go through that again, ever again, Lorraine!

Sorry. And again, I do accept all the apologies you offer as well as I offer to you but the DAMAGE is irreparable.

I HUNGER for you but I can no longer HAVE YOU!

John, I hate that Lorraine!
*I solemnly swear that there will be no hint of
that disturbing scenario again. I overdid things
those last few days. Ask anyone who has ever seen
that behavior in me. They would be in disbelief.
I hate that person! I wouldn't, for the life of me,
want to put you through that wringer again.*
*I want you so badly right now, even in my
periods. I want to be your CUNT.*

Her pleading seemed heart-felt but even after one month only, of being together and breaking up, twice, something did not ring true. Even at this early moment, it seemed that he was talking (writing) to two people.

What we are going to do, Lorraine, is first calm down. I need peace and solitude. I shall hit the maelstrom of international travel again on Thursday. Between now and then, NOTHING! I need time, space and peace, to think! I will, however, compose what is in my mind. It will be wide ranging – from rules construction to other stuff that you and I seem to understand but to which we have both approached clumsily: you smoking weed before trying to torture me in Kenema (disaster). Us fucking Kate (delicious then backfiring); the following day of total HORROR, ending in (damn it) exquisite fucking and love-making.

Stop smoking, no weed and cut down on booze.

Until my letter on Sunday; let me have some time, please.

I will do as you want. I will wait. I will find a destination. Enjoy your stay.

***

I have just asked forgiveness from everyone. Listen to me, I am broken. Do you care? Is it worthy?

I care because I triggered something awful and frightening from within you. I have already apologised.

Your new picture is attracting much interest from the number of hits. I cannot sleep properly because of that awful Sunday.

Take care.

John.

How do profile pictures generate hits?

No, you triggered something beautiful in me. It's why I am in love with you so much! I want to learn more (without drama), enjoy more with you, I cannot find another you. I have not been able to sleep, with all the stress of losing you and I'm having the worst cramps. I am not talking to anyone. No one knows anything...

Let's get something fucking clear, you walking cunt! Your new picture appears whenever you send a Gmail message. It is alluring and, as of now, I click on it and... it has had 625 hits and you have one follower. It's in the Gmail circle system. It was posted the day after our horror show. If it was the other way round, you would be freaking out yet again; going berserk even and lashing out with the wildest accusations!

Apart from the first weekend, you told me at some point in each following weekend, that it was finished. Now, I am simply scared of you and for you. I don't like smoking and I can't afford to sustain you in the level of wine consumption.

I'm so sorry. I know and I KNOW, I shall never find another like you. I thought that five years ago then YOU PROVED ME WRONG, YOU CUNT! What am I to fucking do?

You can call me a cunt! I put the picture on my profile because I had time on my hands. Not for any other reason. I don't know what it means to get hits. I have said, I don't want to be THAT again. Can't I show you that? Am I not worth it after what we have done together? Forgive me, we found us. Let's work on it. I will quit smoking for you, for me. I promise. Please don't be mean to me. I am doing a great job of that already. You said you would never let me go.

I call you a 'walking cunt' as a recognised form of endearment between YOU and ME! Never letting you go was before that awfulness. I remain genuinely scared, Lorraine!

Is this part of my punishment, John? Let me know because I will take it. Did I mean nothing to you, John?

We made love the whole night till morning. After the fight, we promised each other a lot, we meant it. At least, I meant it. I was so ready to face the music, making compromises for normalcy, changing my habits (believe me). I realised what an ass I had been all along.

Let me remind you of what happened.

When you came in the evening, you were fatigued from lack of sleep, working the whole day, the horror of Sunday constantly in your head and you thought I was in a fighting mood. I didn't want to fight you, stop you or shout at you. All I could do was watch, take very angry strides, walking away and ready to push me away if I dared stop you. I had vowed earlier that I would not want those ugly scenes again, no matter what. So all I could do was watch your back as you disappeared, I could not even cry, I was so exhausted and all I could do was sit in the darkness, feeling very sick. I had done this to the only person that I would never want to hurt. I pushed my limits, alcohol wise and indulgences. I like the original idea we had before the horror home and occasional dinners. That would have worked out fine, contrary to what I have shown you, I am not a party animal. Everyone around me knows that. Going out with you the first time was like a first in two months for me. It's simply not me, I cannot do two days of drinking, I do not metabolize alcohol fast enough, so drinking on day two always messes me up and this time it was day three of excessive binge drinking. I got messed... I messed big time and would just like a break. I want to show you the real me. Wouldn't that make for interesting twists to your previous relationships? We will take oaths. I am your whore. I yearn for gentler exciting words.

Is this part of my punishment, John?

Let me know because I will take it. IF YOU LIKE, THEN YES!

John's first thought was that 'the lady doth protest too much'. Then he cited her question.
'Did I mean nothing to you, John?' FUCK IT, LORRAINE! YOU MEAN EVERYTHING, IDIOT!

'I am your whore. I yearn for gentler exciting words'.

THESE WORDS YOU SHALL GET ON SUNDAY. IF YOU'RE A GOOD GIRL, YOU MIGHT EVEN WAKE UP TO THEM BUT I NEED TWO DAYS – THE REST OF TODAY AND TOMORROW...

I will be good. I promise.

***

You are my fucking slut and I am your male whore (BUT CAN IT ALL REALLY WORK WITHOUT YOUR VIOLENCE TOWARDS ME?).
No airport; none of that. A couple of weeks later, you having selected a weekend location, that's the first time we MAY see each other again.

Oh, my god! Okay, rest some, I will do the same. I will wait for your letter. I WILL NOT BE VIOLENT. *Stop punishing me. I will not be okay with you being in Freetown and not seeing you.*

Let's get away; no booze, weed, and so on. Be honest and make adult decisions. Life is too short. I will look for a location. I will let you know. Meanwhile, if it's not too much to ask, please, let it just be only me until we have met?

You know why I hurt stupidly, because I don't cheat when in a relationship, have never and will never and would like to think that it could be reciprocated; do me that one favour?

I have been violent only once on that horrid day. When in Kenema, I swear, I tried to slap you as you did me. It was awkward because it was a first for me. I was not violent before! We both wanted it to explore the darker side of matters.

We owe each other to see each other.

Don't you get an inkling of how ready I am to work this out? I have never said "I love you," not in a long time, but then I met you! I got overwhelmed! I fucked up!

There is no question about anyone else! Who else, for heaven's sake? Yours is the fuck of the century and that's the tip of the beautifully emotional and pornographic possibility. A POSSIBILITY, LORRAINE, that we shall discuss, deeply and sincerely.

OK. I will wait, I will work on myself meanwhile. Enjoy your rest and solitude.

Unfortunately for me: YOU ARE ON MY MIND, CONSTANTLY. As I appear to be on yours!

Finally, some good news; my period (which is flowing like a river this time... too much shock?) seems to sooth my rawness away. You are on my mind every minute.

4.

I know what you want from me. What I need to know is; "Can I place my heart, my wildest dreams, my fears and everything in between, in your hands? Can you love, thrill and protect me as I would aspire to do for, to and with you?"

Against all his better judgement, he was succumbing to all that was sexy, wild, pornographic and at times, genuinely (but rarely), just fun. It was interesting from John's psychological perspective. He professed the need for emotional safety but his thinking was dominated by sex; deep, wild and at times, beautifully disgusting. The thrilling version.

You can place your heart in my hands. I want to give you everything there is that makes us closer. You can trust me, if you let me, without prior ugliness tainting it. I want to love wholeheartedly. I still do but with a different pair of glasses. I want to be your protector, your first resort. I want you to trust me.

OK! You did not answer the blunt question about Smith (her friend in J'burg – she threatened to go and fuck him, in her post-threesome fury), the Viking (her most recent partner, who had offered her a visa to Sweden – I'll fuck him and then I'll tell you) and your ex (the jerk she had a torrid threesome with that went wrong as well – "I'll fuck him, you bastard").

I'm going to stop now and start composing the message for your Sunday reading...

I did not talk to any. I have not talked to anyone on the phone and disabled my Facebook account the day you walked out on me, I could not handle anyone. I have since cringed from even thinking that I told you those ugly made up things. That tantrum was not pretty. Was the question 'if I talked or contacted any', the answer is a resounding NO! Would I like to? NO! I am sorry for trying to make you jealous.

There is only one way you are PERMITTED to make me jealous! When you are kissing a woman's mouth or licking her cunt with blind enthusiasm - but eventually bringing me into the picture! Understood?

Understood!

... and on that happy (and I hope, genuinely understanding) note, let me return to changing – washing all the spare beds in this house, which have not been changed in months; mainly because none have been slept in. Just the need to freshen things up.

I still have oceans of thoughts concerning you – the potential for eliminating fear included. Please rest a little easier tonight. Try to be easy on me. It's been a tough few days of nothing but turmoil and beating myself. I am not violent. Please don't think me so. Try to remember the great times. There were many more than the negatives. I will let you get to your chores. I will have a long shower and get to bed and watch something easy for my mind then sleep, now that hope is on the horizon.

Take care.

The truth was that this excessively erotic woman, with appearance and dress sense to confirm the fact, was violent, both verbally and physically. It was a drunken fury. It was horrible; again, the worst twenty-four hours in his adult life. It was sickening and yet...

You really do have some poetic phrases: '... that hope is on the horizon'. Let's see how my letter unfolds. I have vague notions but nothing concrete. I was, however, disappointed when you agreed, then declined to have an HIV test with me, particularly when you then revealed that the last time you did so was with your ex. Anyway, just one of my other insecurities. Why do you want me, Lorraine? Why do you think you love me, Lorraine? Why do you lavish compliments about my appearance upon me? Why do you think others look at me with desire (I am blind to that) - even that Amazon in that green dress. (The green dress adorned a large woman who was sitting on her kitchen worktop, with her panties exposed and her breasts almost dropping out of her dress, drinking, smoking and joking with Lorraine and her flat-mate. John was oblivious to the asserted 'looking at you'.) Just WHY, Lorraine? In God's name, WHY?

Yes, I know I disappointed you when I did not go for the test. I was a bit scared, especially when I realised that we had fucked Kate without protection (that lazy third fuck of yours - admittedly at her insistence) and we did not seem to mind it. I wondered about you. I did about me. I can't remember the last time I did not use a condom and they have not been many occasions, believe it or not. I got scared and I was being my stubborn self; no other explanation.

Why do I want you, you ask? It's so obvious! My sisters agreed and my few friends agree. You are my kind of man: handsome, tall, lean, healthy, assured, very cocky when it suits, demeanor that shows class because you made me feel like I was the only one in the room wherever we were. I felt so good when coming from the plane and you took all our bags in one arm and held me protectively by the other hand. It felt so dreamy, my handsome knight and you have done several of them and it never fails to make my heart flutter. I love talking with you. We talk about everything, we laugh so much, so hard together; so many other little things. I am fighting for this because you are a treasure. I know this and I messed it all up.

I genuinely fell in love with you when you came to my bed the first time, hugged me hard and you were shaking so hard with feeling. I remember having this overwhelming inexplicable flood of emotions. I wanted to hold you longer, kiss your tears, do anything to make you happy (ironic - ha!).

You make me feel safe. You make me feel wanted. You make me lose my inhibitions but in a gentle way. I see you walking straight towards me with lust and love. I fell in love every moment of those times. I love you because I feel like I can trust you with us. If we work this out, you would do what was best for us. I truly believe that. I have listened to your family stories and it clearly shows that you can be trusted. I don't really think it would be the same if you had a hateful relationship with your ex-wife, so that shows that you are a reliable man.

You are attractive, period.

If we don't work out, at least I met you.

Why do I lavish you with compliments? Because they are true. How you do not know? That baffles me.

I was lucky to meet someone who wears his clothes well, takes care of his body and is proud of it. Why would I miss to compliment you?

I am very scared for the first time in a long time!

You remember that time you brought me a piece of bread and you were at the door. I came to meet you with my arms wide open and you hugged me so tightly and exhaled so deeply, like it's all you needed. That moment there is when I knew for damn sure that I loved you (even if I was engaging in foolhardy behaviour).

I would rather not think of other women wanting you. You want me jealous? Why?'

DOZY WOMAN. I do not want to make you feel jealous. I am unaware of what you tell me, that other women look at me...

I am wondering. Is it an act of love to cling to you when you clearly do not want me. Will you love me the same? Will you respect me after all this? Can you truly forgive and move on positively and stronger?

STOP THIS! Let me work through some thoughts. You shall read on Sunday.

The women look at you absolutely and I get a certain thrill from it, I just wouldn't want you taken from me. You are hot! Get used to it! Okay, Sunday will absolutely do. Till then...

CUNT! BITCH! Play your cards right and I shall NEVER be taken from you! IDIOT!

I am your only cunt! I will please you!

...and on that scintillating note, my manhood rises to you in salute! Rest well. My composition to you is taking shape. Sleep deeply. I will have my first relaxed night since... The fact that I am actually writing to you speaks volumes. Something is going on and I have to work it out. Sunday, Lorraine, Sunday!

Until Sunday comes, I wish you peace and may you find the answers that you are looking for.

You are anything but boring (not so many of you around). You are so attractive in so many ways that makes my heart melt every time I see you. You are the most gentle, caring gentleman. You make me feel like a teenager. I glow. You have said before, you do that to me.

I love your brain. I love your heart; gentle and brittle. I love your taut body. I love what you do with it to me. You are beautiful! I love how you get me a cup of tea in bed in the morning; makes me feel loved. I love being seen with you. I am so proud to have met you.

I'm taking a break from my epistle to Lorraine. With luck, you'll get something tomorrow...

My heartbeats are so irregular and fast! I will just cross my toes and fingers... and now my heart beats harder when I have just checked the meaning of 'epistle'! Very worried indeed.

Heavens! What *does* epistle mean? I thought it meant 'letter' – but in the biblical context.

Okay, didactic? Okay, I am just scared (and not in a 'Shades of Grey' way... Or should I?).

I'm still writing, reading, changing, adjusting, trying to work out my one mind. At this moment, I do not know how the letter will end. This whole business – Lorraine, John, Lorraine and John, John and Lorraine – is very complex.

Oh my! This will be a restless night! I wish you could just let me have it. I will wait though. I want to be a coward and just say fuck it!

5.

This is not a conventional letter. It is a stream of consciousness. I do not know how it will end. I use it as a way of clearing my thoughts about everything. It is now just after five p.m. What is to be written – what is to be revealed or what is to be uncovered – has been going in and out of my head all day but without conclusion. Please don't jump to the end to see what the result is. If there is one, it will be embedded in the text so that you will be compelled – or at least encouraged – to read every word. As the 'stream' unfolds, you will notice that there are no paragraphs. It is simply one long, solid piece of text... of thought. I know you are in contact with your ex and others who have expressed interest in you, Smith included. This you are entitled to; it is part of your history. Equally, I am entitled; it is part of my history. I sleep in a single bed in my house here; it's in the workroom. Others would call it a study. It has all my college books to the front. There's a picture of my PhD graduation pose; my hair is black. I have not slept in the marriage bed since leaving NY in May 2009, when Moira came back from school early to wave me (her daddy) goodbye. My heart broke at that moment. My remorse for what I have done to my family remains. You have suggested that I should move on and maybe I should. The question is, what am I to 'move on' to? Violence: my first memory was when I was six. I was picked up from my bed. It must have been in the middle of the night.

I was taken to a stone-floored kitchen. My granny owned a small private hotel; the prestigious address of 3 Royal Terrace, in a splendid Georgian part of Edinburgh. There was broken glass and sauce bottles strewn all over the floor. I remember hearing the crunching glass under foot. I was carried out to a taxi; the air was freezing. There had been an almighty fight between my father (still in his twenties then) and his mum (my granny – probably in her mid-forties). Next thing I can remember was sleeping in a strange bed in a strange apartment with my father and stepmother. Sometime later, we were in social housing on the southern edge of the city. I would be sent out on a Sunday to buy cigarettes for the parents. I hated doing so because I couldn't speak and I hated (and still do hate) the smell of cigarettes. I was sent to a special needs school, which saved me. I was sixteen and it was the Christmas period. By then, we had an apartment in the city again. My father had separated from my stepmother. One evening, he had a party with work colleagues. I was in my room, avoiding the noise, booze and banter. Then I heard glasses smashing and my father yelling. "Get that fucking Catholic out of my house... just as bad as the fucking Jews!" By that age, I had worked out what was right and wrong. I came out. He was being physically – forcibly – restrained by three of his colleagues. It was a sickening sight. The last time I saw him was one like that – in a post-inebriated state – was three years later. He had been away on a binge for two days and two nights over the New Year. He had persuaded my stepmother (I only ever called him by her first name) to come back but the attempt at reconciliation was short lived. I walked past him on the street. She had already left that morning, for ever. I was leaving for good that evening, for the overnight train to London; my first day in the army. Betty (my stepmother), was an attractive woman. The previous night, I could have lost my virginity to her (described in *The Early Years*). Whether physical or emotional violence, it was still violence. The next experience of overt violence was with you. I vowed to myself that if I ever got through that day and night, I would never see, speak to or in anyway, be in contact with you again. Your threats were unspeakable and I believed each one: whether fucking Smith or a stranger to get rid of the idea of me, to the police and stuff in between. Threatening to cut yourself and trying to grab my phone and confirm your suspicions just added to the horror of the whole thing. The trigger for this all to happen may have been me but it was an inadvertent act. The fear was and remains that whether you protest or not, that potential in you seems to be there, just below the surface. That night in Casablanca, the strip club (when you walked away from me for no reason that I could understand), then that last place, where you forced me to drink whisky ("let yourself go!") you kept telling me, was awful. I don't do these things. I don't drink the way you do. Frankly, I can't afford to sustain that level of consumption either and I won't. Did you make peace with Kate? It would be a pity for you to lose a business partner which seems to work well. Even as I write this portion, I feel my anxiety levels rise. You scare me. I am afraid of you. I'm afraid of what you might do if ever there was an opportunity for you to misunderstand a word, an expression, a hand movement or whatever else might trigger the vitriol within you, again. This I cannot deal with. I won't deal with. My heart and indeed my body cannot manage such things. Then I type the word body and that triggers another stream of thought. You compliment me in the extreme about mine. As for yours? Sometimes, actions speak louder than words. The last time we fucked and made love – both so powerfully – tells you what I think of yours. B the way, you may want to delete the alluring picture on Gmail connections and simply send it to me. Was it taken on the 8th or much earlier? It was posted on the 8th, the day I was negotiating for my future in Sierra Leone after only three hours sleep and a previous day and night to forget. But the trigger to that awfulness. Let's think for a moment. You spoke, on our last fucking night, of your dream of an eighteen-year-old… Whether that, Kate, or another of her (your) age, there are certain rules that should be honoured. If I was offering the stages of such an encounter, my thoughts would be as follows: after talking and a little drink to help all parties to relax, hand holding, gentle caressing and so on, the first contact would be mouth-to-mouth kissing between Lorraine and the guest woman (as was done, to great ice-breaking success with Kate). I then joined in, which was also good. Clothes came off. You started kissing and sucking her. It looked hot and I was jealous (in a good way, if there is such a thing). Then I found myself inside her. I cannot remember if you encouraged it or if I just drifted into it but that's where things went wrong. In future (if indeed, it were ever to happen again), it should be you taking hold of me and placing my cock firmly inside you. Not only would that ensure our primary connection but also it would (or should) 'turn on' the third party. What then follows could be anything but with you orchestrating our pleasure, whether simply together, with her watching, or with her involved, whoever 'her' might be. However, I'm almost sure that this corrected approach is now of academic interest; that its possibility of happening again – the threesome I mean – is remote but let's see. I have one more theme to explore. I try and keep myself strong, for myself. I have pride in physical

51

appearance (nothing to do with attempting to be handsome; you either are or you aren't). The same for a woman; physically, she's either beautiful or she's not. You are and I think you know it; not in a vain way. You are just aware and you carry yourself – and dress yourself – accordingly. I admire that. Yet there is more. Your nakedness is so smooth and inviting. You know it and when you transmit those willing signals, I pounce on you, take you from behind (delicious), suck your cunt and pussy (I can't get enough of both; the taste). I suck your pussy – cunt – juice and bring it back to your mouth. You consume and leave a little for me. You drink my cum (and leave a little for me). You take me and I take you. We take each other and sometimes I shudder at the ultimate emotion of it all. Pornographic, explicit, sensual, erotic and emotional sex. At times it overwhelms me. You have acknowledged this. We started the wrong way round – 'flights of fantasy and exploration but no LTR'. This of course, within a few hours, proved to be entirely wrong. We had leapt to the emotional plane and yet, we were saddled with the original concept. It backfired in Kenema, booze, weed, me tied up, then disaster. You lay in bed later and told me "we're finished!" In so many words, you told me the same thing in each of the following three weeks (weekends) then in our last, it was me telling you! A week or so earlier, I felt I was being used. I was 'an appendage'. I was a mere convenience. The central question really is, what do I want in a relationship with a woman for the rest of my life? The other question is what does Lorraine want in a relationship with a man for the rest of her life (or indeed his life, if he is twice her age)? I think it is easier for John to answer the question for Lorraine, in the spirit of friendship. Lorraine wants a man she can believe in, totally and completely. This belief starts at friendship level; she gets on well with him, can laugh with him, can have disagreements with him but never to threaten their basic bond. Then comes love. She wants to love and be loved, without question. She wants to adore and be adored, without question. She wants to know that her man hungers for her at all times possible, in all places possible. Lorraine just wants that totality of an emotional bond – friendship, love and sexual hunger, to be satisfied, again and again and again. But where is that extra dimension, that which separates Lorraine and her man from all other potential men and all other couples she is aware of. The suggestion is this and it is a serious suggestion, alluded to but never quite given conceptual clarity. Lorraine no longer needs to go through a series of 'fantasies' to satisfy her curiosity. She can 'live' all that she desires in the erotic and pornographic world with the potential man that she has come to express love and passion for and with. If I am right so far, then good. If I am wrong, please correct me. At one point in bed, you spoke of organising an orgy; a gang-bang. I think that would frighten me. It would distract too much from you and me as the central fuckers in the group activity... So what does John want? Funnily enough, he wants precisely what Lorraine wants with one condition; that she genuinely copes with his insecurities to the point that over time and because of her love, care and affection, these fears of his eventually disappear. How and why? The love she showers upon him – her belief in him – slowly extracts all his pain and uncertainties, started when he was five, so that he becomes whole and confident in the one area he is not: emotionally, hence the charge of, "I feel like an appendage." Yet all these sentiments are based on the possibility of now; the next month (if he returns with a new contract) or the next couple of months (when he returns to pack up his belongings because no contract has been signed). Then optimistically, what then, beyond the year? Lorraine hates planning. John loves planning. John has made the following clear. He is not the normal white man in Sierra Leone with money to throw at pleasure. He has his estranged family to support, a large mortgage in the USA to sustain and modest personal habits to fund: rent, food and the occasional pleasure, a meal out with wine for her and (now) beer for him. At some point, there will have to be some down-sizing in a year or two then other possibilities might come to the fore. John's personal life is modest except for one thing. Lorraine has generated a sexual appetite in him that has lain dormant for years (except in his earlier and sometimes very powerful writing). It has been there and has been relieved occasionally through hand-jobs at the end of massages, while not in a relationship; always a sad and unfulfilling end. Then Lorraine appears. He can't get enough of her; he pounds her, enters her slowly, has now taken her asshole as well, at her insistence (as she has his) and wonders what to do next; in friendship, in love, in sex, in the pursuit of barriers being pushed to one side in pursuit of the possibilities that she often speaks of and he listens to with relish. You must understand what you are dealing with. You must understand me. You must understand yourself. Above all, you must understand you. You must try and work through all that triggered your fears that exploded that day and night. You must feel safe and happy within yourself. You must know that whatever pain might hit you in future, from whatever source, you shall cope in a calm and intelligent way. Again, I swore to myself that I would never come near you again, by phone, by e-mail or personally. Yet here I am, exposing myself to Lorraine yet again after three weekends of you telling me "we're finished" and me telling you the same last Monday evening; and this is only Saturday and we're banging away at each other emotionally yet again, trying to find a way to get to each other's heart in safety. It's safety that now comes to the fore. What does that mean? For you, I think it means feeling totally secure and unthreatened – that there is no possibility of betrayal. Failure because of honest endeavour that proves that things just won't work is another matter entirely. Do you know what absolute joy it gives me to take you to bed, when we know we are going there, in essence, to sleep, that I put my arms around you, hold you and maybe flirt with you, my cock responding and moving towards your ass... Do you not understand what that essential embrace does for me? I wonder? It is that embrace, that delicate touch (before whatever happens, even if nothing) that gives me such joy, such a feeling of elation. Why did you threaten all that but that's past. We must now look to a possible future. What does that mean? I think it means starting again. I think it means that we know who we are and what we want. I think it means that I shall stop attempting to plan. Instead, I shall seek to build upon solid foundations. That might mean meeting in town and talking, looking into each other's eyes. It certainly means an HIV test. If you can do it together with your ex, you can certainly get off your arse and do it with me – particularly because of your reaction to Kate's smears of blood. Once we've proved to each other that we are free of all diseases, we shall have no more fears because (and I mean because), when we were together at first, I thought I had arrived and that I would never need to find another woman, that I had found her at last (despite your protestations that I was manipulating you, that you were an experiment and so on and so forth). Idiot and again idiot! So, on that revealing note, recognise, just try and recognise why, after that hell we went through last weekend, I am still here, typing into the wee small hours to try and convey to you something that could be wonderful, or could turn into another hell. Either way, easy stages, day by day, week by week, slowly feeling our way (emotionally and sensually) to a point where the idea of not going to bed to sleep and not waking up – me grabbing coffee and offering you tea – is simply not an option. I cannot put it plainer than that. There is much in this 'not a conventional letter'. I want you to read and re-read. I want you to take your time. I want you to think and think hard. I want you to realise the age difference between us. I want you to acknowledge that I will not abandon my estranged family. I also want you to know that I want you to be clothed, fully, scantily and naked, completely. I want to wear an apron for you and nothing else (because you seem to like it). I want you to drool for sex. I want you to open your legs and beg my tongue to embrace the lips of your pussy before plunging deeper. I want you to masturbate in front of me and for me, letting the drip, drip on to my lips and into my mouth. I want you to continue wanting me to spit on you. I want you to spit on me. I want your passion. I want it for me and only me. I want to give you my passion, to spend it all on you and no other. I need no other. I want no other except, through the additional pleasures you conjure up and I agree to be part of. I need everything. I want everything. What that means remains unclear but sleeping and waking as often as possible is a central feature; you beside me (or on top of me) and me beside you (and on top of you). Talk love, talk dirty! I want it all. Think hard, think slowly and carefully. Understand yourself. Understand the possibility of me with you. Understand what that means in the world of living reality. The words are now for you to express. I am simply going to delete everything I have received from you and start again.

6.

Thank you! I had a very restless night waiting for this letter, I have read and re-read it a dozen times already. I spend the whole day replying then just now when I was trying to proof-read the draft, I just had to accidentally delete everything, arghh. I will try to reply in the best way I know how, I am sure you will understand.

1.)'...I know you are in contact with your ex and others have expressed interest in you, Smith included'. As I have told you before, there is no issue with any of my exes. The last one tries once in a while, not hard enough though because he already knows that I am a sailed ship. He knows I met you. There has never been any danger there. Smith and I have had a good friendship, supportive actually. We have never had an affair. We would never and that's why we trusted each other with our mutual love of getting away from grumpy partners. He has harmlessly flattered and always ended with "I'm joking!" I just wanted to hurt you at my most helpless moment, and I chose that.

2.)'...equally, I am entitled; it's part of my history'. What did you mean by this?

3.)'...it's in the workroom, others might call it a study'. Please take photos. That would melt my heart!

4.)'...my heart broke at that moment, my remorse for what I have done to my family'. I cannot say that I truly appreciate the pain of losing your mother at a very young age and your dad not much later on. We both are from broken families, mums leaving at almost the same age(s) and eloping on our own at a very young age. It clearly affected you deeply. I have caught little glimpses of your young life from the books you had given me. I wish I could truly understand it. I think I do. It's just new, if that's an explanation. I am in sympathy. I know you are emotionally sensitive, if ever I have met one! You wrote that you were shy as a teen (hard to imagine that!) and your fixation, almost sexually to mother figures and it's all connected to the early years. I want to understand you, I would like to know your fears. I want to see you even at your most vulnerable. I want to show you that you can trust me with all your hidden-most - your deepest - emotions. I want to understand everything there is to know. I will not judge. I will view with a mind of someone who cares and would like to know more.

5.) '...The next experience of overt violence was with you'. I will not utter vitriol. I will not engage in violence. I am not violent. I ask of you not to label me a violent person. It's not a nice label and you can't characterize me as violent, can you? All I can do with this tag, is just show you by actions. I really do not want to be around you walking on eggshells, not wanting to trigger 'a walking out' on me because you can't take it. I don't want to change who I am. I don't want to be dull. I don't want to change you. What I want to do and I will do, is stop binge drinking, I will never smoke around you, while working on quitting. I want to do it for myself. I have stopped smoking weed. I was not addicted to it anyway. You do not have to spend money on alcohol for me. It was never a necessity. You will see that part in action too.

6.) '...did you make peace with Kate?'. Yes, I did. It was a mistake to ever include a friend. It's one of the rules when engaging in threesomes. It never works; I know. I am trying to smooth that bad taste in my mouth and I can't because I see her every day and I am getting resentful. I cannot control it. She was coming from another date last night and I felt ill just hearing about it all. I think she's a nymphomaniac. All I could think of is, 'did they use a condom'? I didn't ask. She said I should get over my guilt. She did and moved on. I envy her. I apologized for the saga. When I tentatively talked about the condom and she could see that I was not so pleased, she apologized and said that she did not expose us. I was upset but kept it to myself, just left her and went to my room. I am now truly scared about our HIV tests!

7.)'...you scare me, I am afraid of you, I am afraid what you might do if there's ever an opportunity for you to misunderstand a word, an expression, a movement or whatever else might trigger the vitriol in you'. Again, I am sorry that happened at all. It has happened once in my two day binge. I am I now 'Lorraine the violent?' Again I can only show you with my actions, if you let me.

8.)'...you compliment me in the extreme about my body'. I do so because it's in great shape! You have a handsome face, great skin, you walk tall and straight. I always get thrilled viewing your taut body pounding me oh so beautifully! I love... I love your body!

9.)'...you may want to delete the alluring photo from Gmail connections'. It's already down, I don't know the exact date I put it up, but if you say it was after the horrid day, then I believe you. It had no connection with any event that happened. I spent the whole following day in bed, bored. I must have updated lots of my apps. I had no idea outsiders could see someone's photo and for your information, that photo was taken when I came to your place late at night and you gave me that juicy fucking on the dining table, that exact night. I will send you the photo shortly after being done with this letter. It captures a feeling of deep sensual satisfaction!

10.)'... Let's think for a moment on our last fucking together. You spoke of your dream of an eighteen-year-old; whether that or Kate or another of her (your) age. There are certain rules to be honored'. Don't I know these rules well! There's no question. There will be never another Kate. Friends are not recommended for threesomes. It changes everything. My head is reeling from how I let things just get the way they did. We had not talked about it. Our relationship was as shaky as it could be; wrong time for a threesome - far too early! Now that I have calmed down and have had time to reflect on my actions and why it got where it did, I am coming up with answers that are not so palatable. Maybe I was unconsciously sabotaging the relationship (why would I bring my friend, when I had trauma from a similar incident?). I have been told countless times that

I am a self-saboteur especially when I am afraid of being in love and other decisions in my life. I find it curious that I had the same kind of stage in love. My ex invited a friend, then the condom saga and then the flare up! What are the chances, I did not plan it? I had that strange feeling when after Kenema, you sent me e-Dreams and you accidentally sent me Three Interludes. Imagine my utter shock when I read what had happened when you and your woman then met in Rome and had the exact experience we had in Kenema? Even the words you used. I thought I was losing my mind! There was no way you could have orchestrated what happened in your book. What are we doing and why? I am still trying to figure it out. I am appalled that you would think that this is my usual behavior but who is to blame; you?

Going back to the threesomes. I love the idea, have been in them, have enjoyed some and some have turned out to be not so good. They say that you should never indulge in threesomes when on shaky ground, emotionally. Heavens, we had only just started. It should have been discussed and given time for the idea to grow and be clearly understood that it should be the two in the relationship to enjoy each other with a stranger, as one way of satisfying each other, looking out for each other. I should have used my strength to stop you from fucking without a condom and deal with my ego issues later. I should have protected you and for that I am sorry.

...as I was saying, I love being adventurous, I love the thrill. I love the new and it's been suppressed and as you know, it's not so easy to find many of us out there. I fight for you because in you, I see myself enjoying wild things together, with limits of course. I wish we had these kind of emails before our lust took over.

When and if we find our soft ground together, I would love to re-group, be able to sit down and talk honestly about our desires and fantasies, maybe through emails? I would like to know so much, share so much, the possibilities are numerous I believe.

Yes, I would want to revisit our fantasies and options together and yes, I would like to lick and eat an eighteen-year-old pussy with you, together, for us, and have heaven fun while doing it!

11.)'...I felt like I was being used, I was an appendage, a mere convenience'. That really saddens me. I wish we had that relationship where you could tell me how you felt at that moment. I wonder what times and why would I have you around for a mere convenience? Who does that? That is sad because until you told me, it was never as you thought.

12.) '...what does Lorraine want in a relationship with a man for the rest of her (or indeed his life, if he is twice her age)'. Total and complete love and loyalty, no betrayal, not even a possibility!

13.) '...Lorraine no longer needs to go through a series of 'fantasies' to satisfy her curiosity. She can 'live' all her desires in the erotic and pornographic world with the potential man that she has come to express love and passion for and with)'. My heart sang when I read and re-read that paragraph. I have you back my love!

I want to love you properly.

14.) 'What does John want? Funnily enough, he wants what Lorraine wants, with one condition; that she genuinely copes with his insecurities to the point and overtime and because of her love, care and affection, these fears will eventually disappear'. Baby, I want to understand your pain. I want to understand your fears. I want to always be there when you need me. As I said before, I want to be your first resort. I know how to be that. I care but I have to understand what it is that you are going through. I will help you get over your fears. Help me get over mine too. I will do my utmost to protect you. I will love you.

15.) 'We must now look to a possible future'. I cannot wait to start on that. I do not want to change myself, apart from demons that came out last weekend and the changes I have put in place. I truly do not want to change myself. I do not want to be afraid of messing when having a conversation, I do not want to bring up the past when talking about stuff that had nothing to do with the past, I do not want to be called violent at any disagreement we might have.

I do not want John to change. If planning is what you do... heck, maybe I should have borrowed a leaf from you; that threesome would then never have happened! All I can ask of you is to never involve me in a triangle relationship. I cannot bear to be cheated on. I know the pain and that's why I don't do it; don't do that to me.

I ask for an honest relationship. I have felt that you have been up to something. I don't know how right I was but something was up (part of my slow simmer). I don't know how right I was, but it bothered me for a week. I watched you without you seeing so many times. I wanted you to see the questions on my face, to reassure me and it kept getting worse. You know all the traps and stuff. Then the icing on the cake was the threesome. After binge drinking, a perfect disaster recipe!

What is the fun of being in a hide-and-seek relationship? Nothing. Just causes anxiety; turns you into a psycho for a day. I truly despise games.

It's the reason I crave an open relationship, with strict rules, where we can enjoy other stuff but still be in a very secure and loving relationship. We then win both ways. I cannot wait for when we start having these conversations. I am already turned on.

16.) 'Once we have proved to each other that we are free from all diseases, we shall have no more fears because (and I mean because) we were perfect together at first. I thought I had arrived and I would never need to find another woman; that I had found her at last'.

Please elaborate? Were you with anyone else?

17.) '...easy stages, day by day, week by week, slowly feeling our way (emotionally and sensually)'. I miss those moments when you would bring me tea in bed, smelling so fresh and looking so delicious. Yes, I would like to take it easy. I want to understand and know you, contrary to what you believe. I have no desire to be seen at Bintumani. I had hoped that you still had plans to move but I guess we are back to square one. I will not feel okay or comfortable in the least, coming to meet you there, so that's a NO, but we can always meet for coffee and tea. We cannot have all the answers now. We will see where we are headed, I hope.

18.) '...I want you to realize the age difference between us. I want you to acknowledge that I will never abandon my estranged family'. I do realize your age. Unfortunately it's what I choose and feel most comfortable to be around. About your family: I would never in a thousand years think of interfering, complaining and bitching about. That's your family and you protect them the best way you know how. How would I come in? I admire the arrangement that you have in place and admire you as a man for doing that.

19.) '...I want you to be clothed, fully, scantily and naked, completely...understand me, understand yourself, understand what you are getting yourself into'. I know myself. I trust myself and make stupid decisions as everyone else does. I cope with my mistakes when pointed out. I fall in love like everyone else. I fell in love with you unexpectedly. All I know is, I want to lay where you lay your head. I want to hear your voice as much as I can. I want to hold hands with you when I can, kiss your beautiful mouth whenever I have a chance. I want to make love to you; proper love, to kiss and savour every inch of your skin. Don't ever stop spitting on me, slapping and spanking me, fucking my cunt like you would want to tear it in two. We are two passionate beings and we are good when we are in bed. We are wonderful animals. It is Perfection.

I miss you so much and I regret that instead of chatting excitedly over the internet, we are trying to get back together, tentatively, lest we mess up again. I wish it was not so because I miss my John and Lorraine is terribly sorry.

I hope I have managed to reply, at least satisfactorily. I am just happy that we have a chance together and can only hope that this time round will be a happy one. I will send this, then will shortly send the 8th day photo.

7.

I just had to add this. John, I told you about me and my unresolved issues. I tend to keep things that bother me hidden and repressed; a very dangerous habit. Indeed, it is part of the reason the horror day happened in the first place, when I was in my crazed alcoholic state. I told you that I would leave you and you could have Kate. You readily agree; happily actually. What should I take from that?

Would it hurt if it was you in my shoes? Hence the question, would you leave me and be with someone we had a threesome with? That will be a worry if you do not answer satisfactorily. I have feelings of resentment towards her that I cannot explain. Our clumsiness made me so afraid for myself and my ego, I do not know if I can truly get past that with her. I don't know why I am giving you a free pass. Let me tell you how I felt when I watched you fucking her, completely gone, no condom. When it dawned on my fuzzy mind what was happening, I felt like my heart had been ripped away. I had this jealous rage that only an inebriated woman could express the best way she knew how. I was very upset. I could not think clearly. You felt like a stranger and her, a witch. I could not breath. I knew I was completely drunk but saw what was happening (I have never been this incensed and drunk before). I do not know why I have to get drunk when I get naughty thoughts in my head but never being mean when drunk; that is almost unheard of. Why were you ready to take her on?

I want to love. I want to show you how caring I am, how affectionate I am. I want you to trust me. I want us to explore beyond our boundaries together; that I can let you fuck another woman while I languidly lay back and enjoy watching beautiful bodies fucking. I want you to watch me fuck a girl till she screams in orgasm. I would like us to have several women over for a nude dinner night and treat you like a king or we, your slaves; erotic surprises and games but it all boils down to security. I would make you the happiest man if you promised fidelity and love in all its forms. Then it will be Me and You. I am yours, if you are mine.

Write back, I miss you.

Sometimes I write as I speak, so fast. Please forgive how I write, I feel terrible, sending a not well written letter to an accomplished writer.

My gorgeous Lorraine,

NO! There has been nobody else – whether while we were together or since. I have no ambitions to be with any other, except through us. I conceded to the possibility of Kate because I thought it was part of the package. I was wrong. I would like you to gently and quietly let that go.

Your letter in response has been astonishing! I am proud of you in that I am proud of the woman I want to be with – OK? I've said it. Through everything, I write and declare in words, "I want to be with you in total trust and honesty."

This is a short message because I have stuff to attend to in London today, including seeing a dying 'aunt-in-law' in hospital, going to a movie and hosting my daughter to dinner this evening in CBD, before returning. I'm travelling both ways by train, so I will be able to enjoy a glass or two of beer (no red wine, definitely no red wine!).

Stop fretting about the HIV test. As I suggested on our very first day together, it marks a commitment to each other, And I WANT that COMMITMENT to each other!

Let's revert to the original idea about Bintumani. We will inch our way forward for the next three months; meanwhile, you are to find nice places for the occasional weekend away and possible alternative accommodation – clear?

I'll take pictures of my workroom, where I sleep. If everything works, you'll get them tomorrow.

He then re-read part of her message. It was sublime. It resonated deeply. He had to read it yet again...

'I want to love, I want to show you how caring I am, how affectionate I am. I want you to trust me. I want us to explore beyond our boundaries together; that I can let you fuck another woman while I languidly lay back and enjoy watching beautiful bodies fucking. I want you to watch me fuck a girl till she screams in orgasm, I would like us to have several women over for a nude dinner night and treat you like a king or we your slaves, with erotic surprises and games but it all boils down to security. I would make you the happiest man if you promised fidelity and love in all its forms. Then it will be Me and You. I am yours, if you are mine.

This was his idea of *Perfection*.

My god, Lorraine! Am I not yours? Why am I draining my mental and emotional strength writing that 'non-conventional letter' if I am not yours? I am YOURS in total fidelity and love. Take care of me in all things and I shall take care of you...

Love and more,

John.

She then reverted, as if the other Lorraine had been triggered back to life.

Thank you for the positive response.

I am not satisfied with Kate's issue. It was not a package, it was clear. I was breaking up with you and you were ready to take her on... remember, we are starting clean, honesty? I can't wait for your letter. I have just realised that I miss you more than I did before. I can't wait for the new us! I hope you enjoyed your dinner with your daughter and had positive catching up on your lives.

I am at home, really frustrated, trying to get hold of my tailors who are playing with my work, trying to find new tailors, nothing much going on here, always at home. I have no desire to go anywhere or have a drink with anyone. I am detoxed completely and now happier that you are with me again.

About Bintumani: I will never be able to step there again, that is just me and I don't think I will change my mind on that. I would rather I let those ugly ghosts sleep, I would never be able to re-enter that place.

About the HIV test: I am literally trembling when I think about it...we will talk when you get here.

I love you, John.

Please, beautiful Lorraine, let the Kate thing go....

Please stop fretting about the HIV test; select the clinic and let's do it. Your mind will be put at rest.

Please stop bothering about Bintumani. Let's move on as originally intended – three months gradual increase together, then BANG!

Over the next two days, I am going to extract all the 'hunger' items you have declared for me. I need to consolidate them anyway; good for morale as well as my self-esteem.

Finally for now, here are four self-explanatory pictures...

Love and more!

Your man!

Wow, sweets!

Your home in England is homey and sweet!

I have been squinting hard trying to ascertain what kind of books and movies are on your shelves. Oh, please take a closer picture of your graduation photo. I would really like to see it. It's beautiful. I am trying to picture what you could be doing.

About Kate: I want to but I cannot let it go until I have answers. If you prefer not to tell me, it's not blackmail, I swear but we will always have it hanging over our heads. Until settled, it's bothering me and I would like you to care that it's bothering me.

I miss you and wish I was in your arms.

Bintumani will never do it for me again, I would need a year of therapy before I do.

We are taking it slow. We will figure things out with time.

Baby!

If you toss me to one side, why should I not seek comfort in another? However, as I said before, I thought it was part of the 'game' and so I agreed. If you can't let this go, then we have a difficulty. One form of perverse therapy would be (a) to repeat the whole thing, (b) to have lots of condoms and (c) for the first bout of fucking to be between you and me – so that (d) we drive her crazy with envy and (e) to get you back to a happy normality about the whole thing. As I said, deliciously perverse.

Stop thinking about Bintumani; history for you and eventually for me too, so relax!

The only sexual pleasure I am getting at this moment (relax again) is after I've been to the toilet and had a crap, I go to the sink, pour warm water and wash my asshole. As part of that, I stick my finger in – right in – to ensure that all is clean (and I imagine for one blissful moment that it is your finger cleaning me out....)

More pictures soon! xxx

Baby,

Honey, you have to have patience even with unpleasant discussions. I am trying to remove the difficulty that we might have in the future. As I told you, unresolved issues. You were ready to move on to my friend - is that a possibility? (Not that she would agree but that's not the point). Would you be attracted to my friend? What if you see her now? I need therapy for this kind of 'betrayal'. In loose terms, it traumatized

*me for a long time before. My self-esteem went
downhill. I had trust issues. I want to know what
goes through your mind. Why you do some stuff
and I want you to know me completely; that
TRUST is the key ingredient to an open, erotic,
pornographic relationship.*

*I would never do a repeat and especially not
with Kate!*

*I miss dipping my tongue into that tight,
smooth asshole, swirl my tongue around wildly
while you lay there with soft moans escaping
you...*

My perverse alternative therapy was just that: perverse, not
perverted! I was not ready to move to your friend. The only way I
can convince you is through action, through behavior, I am yours! If
I saw her now, I would simply greet her as a friend and colleague of
yours, nothing more. This I can do. It's the other side of me. Enjoy
the pictures and the idea of me. I'm off to clear out the garage!

8.

My beautiful Lorraine!

You must understand me in all my complexity as I must understand you. I am what I am as you are. What I am working through now is not a reflection of what has happened to us since we met but what could happen to us in the future. My body and my heart — both with beautifully pornographic tendencies and ambitions — have already been taken over. You know that! It started on the first day! What I am trying to do now is to get my mind to catch up. It will but it needs this time away to get all of you — and all of us — into a correct perspective. What we are embarking upon, a commitment to each other, is profound and even frightening because of its emotional implications. What shape that will take, I do not know yet but it is something I am willing to venture into.

Don't you understand what you have done to me? You have turned me inside out. You have entered my heart. You are for me, the sublimely imperfect being; the imperfection being that awful twenty-four hours which, happily recedes, further and further, as my mind, happily, focuses further and further into the future. Do you understand all this? (And yes, I am imperfect too — I know it). Yet some would say, two negatives make a positive, as in basic algebra; my goodness! Two imperfections make the whole

Perfection? A fanciful hypothesis but let's see how things sail forward, with a light touch on the tiller...

I have been sleeping well here; amazingly, eight hours, without an alarm. I need the sleep. In our last week, I was getting about three hours some nights – YES, the pleasure was worth it...

I feel completely fucking horny for you. Tonight, I'm going to send you a most disgusting message, full of bad language and pornographic ideas. Just thought: I shall start with that scene of you standing astride me in the shower... You are my queen: in emotion, in sex, my walking cunt, my slut and my vessel (literally) for all penetration and desire.

More later, my pornographic angel! (Apart from that brief forthcoming opening scene, I have not written in that style for about ten years. It will be interesting to see if I can still do it!)

John xxx

Why do you like me to be unshaved? You know how I must attack your clit, your pussy, your cunt! Does my growth not scratch your inner thighs and your pussy lips or do you like that feeling of being scratched, being taken, a little pain and discomfort as you are being consumed?

I love you unshaven. My insides tremble when you lick my pussy, your beard stubble scratching my pussy lips. I like it a little rough, like being taken by a sexy relentless Beast!

That five o'clock shadow suits you (you have the looks of a great actor!). You have good, clear, clean skin that the scruffy look makes you look relaxed, so very sexy. It should be your normal casual look.

I can't believe I have met you! Thank you for being you; all of you! More much later from me (I am already composing filth in my mind)!

Your man!

My baby!

I need your help. The attached (excuse the yellow background, which I cannot get rid of) is an extract of some of the things you have written to me recently; all positive. I have underlined a few salient points but the whole thing comes down to a fundamental love that allows for so much more. It's that 'so much more' that needs to be tested and by e-mail during this time of enforced (by my physical absence) reflection. As you state: 'I wish we had these kind of emails before our lust took over.' So, let's have these emails now. Let's write honestly about our desires and fantasies. Let's have 'these conversations' now.

As you also say in the attached: 'I want us to explore beyond our boundaries together...'

What I need your help with is the 'fantasies...' something I was hopeless at when you confronted me at one point in Kenema. Help me to help us go 'beyond our boundaries'. The idea of a nude dinner with women and me being treated like a king or such like, would never occur to me. So help me to help us. Let's get the exploration down in writing so that when I get back to you, all (or at least a great deal) is clear to both of us and agreed by both of us.

Is that OK? If so, please start and I shall try and follow.

'...it's that 'so much more' that needs to be tested and by email during this time of enforced (by my physical absence) reflection. As you state, 'I wish we had these kind of emails before our lust took over'.

I wished for that every time I met you, but it's easier said than done, isn't it? I think emailing is the best medium. I can hide behind my computer and write my real truth to you much easier and I believe we can get to know each other much better this way.

I am totally open-minded. Speaking of which, I forgot to reply to you about the gangbang scenario. I don't ever remember telling you that I would want to have a gangbang. It's not and has never been my desire. I remember saying that I could watch you in a gangbang but I would never be part of it. It just does not turn me on. I would not want that done to me. OK? But I would watch you. I don't know if it would turn me on though.

I am open minded. I don't feel guilty about it. I truly enjoy it and getting older is making me understand and want more from this lifestyle. I met you and I knew I wanted to be dirty with you.

'The idea of a nude dinner with women and me being treated like a king or such like would never occur to me...'

You, with a beautiful mind like yours?

Oh, it could be any scene. It's just the idea of having two or more girls waiting with me for you to come from work: us dressed in skimpy white lingerie and gowns, chilled wine, fruits and cheese laid out. You will open the door and be astounded (it would be a surprise), my kissing you reassuringly, gently tugging you inside, then you recover your cool and I introduce you to the two vixens - Nubians? You give them the standard two, one peck on each cheek but you did not expect the younger one to quickly and gently take both sides of your face and give you a full kiss on your mouth. You were shaken and fully aroused. I have to pry you away for a bit, so as not to rush through the night.

I will take you to the bedroom, undress you slowly without touching your throbbing cock. I will take you by hand to the bathroom where a full tub, steaming with scented bubble bath is waiting. I will gently and soothingly clean you up, kissing you all the time, knowing how excited you are about the night ahead. When I am done cleaning you, I go and ask the girls to join me, to towel you dry. We do and it excites you no end and it shows. We lead you to the living room where we have laid the table for you (now in a gown but draped open) and we all swoon around you, feed and touch you. You would ask us to do anything and we would perform for you, masturbate lick another's pussy and suck your cock rim. You praise us, spit on us, punish us, love us, fuck us, and anal fuck us!

I just made myself horny writing that. I don't know how you writers do it.

I know how I write...does that story make sense?

So many things we can do.

Now I see that I rushed through the writing. I promised to be more patient and proof read before. (And yes, we both need this time apart.)

Tell me your fantasies. Tell me how you truly feel. There are fantasies and there are realities. I just think that in our case, the two can merge into a delicious whole.

Let me embed my replies in your text. My promised 'dirty' scene will come to you later tonight, my time; early tomorrow, yours!

Before I start. How are you, Lorraine? Feeling slightly happier within yourself? Slightly happier about me? Slightly happier with me?

'I am totally open-minded, speaking of which, I forgot to reply to you about the gangbang scenario, I don't ever remember telling you that I would want to have a gangbang...

Then I misunderstood the term 'orgy' – men and women... more than one man equals a 'gangbang' to me and that I cannot take – sorry. I'm the only man with you!

I am open-minded, I don't feel guilty about it. I truly enjoy it and getting older is making me understand and want more from this lifestyle. I met you and I knew I wanted to be dirty with you.

Guilt? Why on earth? What we crave is the most profound reality. Those who deny it deny the essence of life! My god, Lorraine! I want you to be 'dirty with me' and more if that is possible...

'The idea of a nude dinner with women, and you being treated like a king or such like, would never occur to you.' Oh, it could be any scene...
You will quickly reveal my cock and just hold it, leading me away and prepare me for what is to come. By now, there will be pre-cum and you must consume it!

I will take you to the bedroom (then) to the living room where we have laid the table for you, (now in a gown draped open)...You praise us, *spit on us, punish us, love us, fuck us, and anal fuck us!*

This is fantastic! My cock is hard as a rock! You would all masturbate – that is a minimum requirement. The two girls would cum over your face. Punishment. The strongest of the extra girls would be set upon – fake raped by us all – you and the other's tongue in her cunt and clit while my cock slides into her asshole... Then the girls and I would turn on you...

The story makes perfect sense and can be done! Arrange it!
Tell me your fantasies. Tell me how you truly feel. There are fantasies and there are realities.

Here is the difference. With you, every fantasy is a potential reality. We dream about what we want. We convert it to reality because we have found each other and know that in deepest love and deepest trust, all such dreams are ultimately real.

I will arrange it, absolutely! But only when we are in a good place; no rush...we have to be really good, really understand each other, understand the rules and get on with it, have a mind blowing pornographic time!

I am so horny!

P.S. Something funny, when you arrived in England and you wrote and said it was over, a *shocker of course! I tried to understand it all, through that excerpt you sent me, when all possibilities had fizzled out then I remembered that you had brought me your 'toy' and two onions. I calculated that maybe the toy symbolised 'F***k yourself' and the two onions symbolized 'cry me a river'. Was I not messed? And is that not funny? Funny yes but with no symbolism intended; I'm not that clever. You are!*

I need to know what more you need from me - just you and me.

I want to be in a dark restaurant. You are to pretend something has fallen. You go under the table, unzip me, take my cock and suck hard just a few moments but for it to be done!

I am so horny!

Masturbate and tell me later what scene entered your dirty head.

My baby!
My daughter is afraid to go to hospital alone; she hates them; the smell, everything. I leave for London at noon my time and (we) shall see frail aunty one more time.

I leave the house for the airport tomorrow at five fifteen a.m., arriving NY around nine p.m. your time. I'll send a short message confirming safe arrival. Then, I shall let myself absorb the only time of year that I have with the family, all together.

Do you want to influence the appearance of your man through his style of haircut? If yes, I shall restrain myself and wait till I get back and then let you influence matters.

You're a good woman, Lorraine, and you are going to benefit from that ultimate quality!

These e-mails, whether calm (this one) or dirty (the next, in response to your reply), are proving to be heaven-sent. The time to re-construct, to understand, to see and feel into each other's fears and desires is all so important. I shall continue writing and responding while in NY.

Love and more,

Your man xxx

Baby,

I understand your daughter. I feel the same way about hospitals, I am sorry about frail aunty, I hope she is not in pain.

I would love to take you to a hairdresser here but if you are there, wouldn't it be nice for you to cut it where you are used to? I could always take you to the barbershop when it grows back.

I am going to give you breathing time when you are with the family. I understand and so happy for you (But I need to hear from you!).

My buddies are bugging me to join them in Addis - the laborious cross-continent journey. I am feeling so guilty but my excitement waned. If

I don't see my American friend (her sister is getting married), I might not see her again until after her two year contract in Russia. I wish it was when we had planned together. Now I feel blah about the whole trip but I will let you know.

Tons of hugs and kisses!

We will look for someone to watch us, definitely! (Threesomes and other scenes will have to wait till I and we heal completely.) *Agreed!* Where, though? Definitely not my house! *Agreed!* When we go for our weekend getaways? *Agreed!* Probably better, plus we will be leaving 'what's in 'Vegas' back in Vegas, yes? *Agreed!* We can be who we want to be, pleasing, fucking and cumming should be our basic intent when we get away; *most assuredly agreed!*

We have a great deal of healing to get on with, though I am well on my way. This past week has been so important – for both of us!

My first concern is your and my pleasure, with you and me. If anything else happens, that is simply a bonus. It is not, repeat not, the primary concern here! Agreed?

9.

We are in your shower.

"Stand astride me!"

"I can't!"

"Do it for fuck's sake. I need it! I need you!"

Your bladder is actually full because we have been talking for the past hour and drinking lots of water...

"Oh god, it's coming; oh my god..."

...and as it trickles then torrents, you find your enthusiasm for such a thing and aim at my face. I take it then you grab my nose. My mouth opens and you piss directly in. I choke a little at first then slap your hand away. I'm drinking the whole fucking thing; I want it. You're amazed. It finishes. You turn the shower on.

"What did it taste like?" you ask.

"A little like weak whisky."

I suggest it's your turn. You hesitate. I don't push it.

We emerge from the shower, both with towels around our waists. You, topless, is something I cannot stand without reacting.

I take you to the dining table. You know that with the force of movement, you dare not resist. In any case, you don't actually want to.

I push you forward so that you are bent and ready for me. "Don't move!"

You obey.

I bring ties and immediately strap one ankle to the table leg, then the other.

You try standing. I push you back, your breasts being caressed by the table top.

I take one wrist and tie you to the far right leg. I take the other and do the same. You are spread apart. You cannot move. You are ready. You wonder what comes next.

I come to your front. Your face is lying to one side. I kiss you. I spit on you. I wipe the spit in.

"You bastard!" you tell me.

"You mean *you* bastard!" I tell you.

I take my belt off.

The back of your upper thighs look inviting. Smack and smack again.

You groan but it's a groan of masochistic pleasure.

I strike your ass cheeks; one blow on each. It isn't enough. I miss the feel of my hand on you. I slap you and slap you again, hard. The hand imprint comes up. I stop.

I lick your cunt. I lick your asshole. You want more.

I get the baby oil and squirt it over both asshole and cunt.

I place my cock at the entrance to your ass; I sense your nervousness; your tightening with fear. I assure you that there is to be no pain when entering this place. I push in slowly, past the point of resistance than find my cock being consumed by your asshole walls. You are even trying to push yourself against me for deeper penetration.

'What a perfect cunt she is!' my mind tells me.

You want it. You want it hard. I resist.

Eventually, I withdraw slowly. I vanish.

"Where are you? You can't leave me like this!"

I return. I want back into your asshole. You welcome me.

I then put my cock into your cunt.

You realise double penetration; that the strap-on is doing its work. Both your holes are being fucked and soundly so; slowly and deeply. It takes about ten minutes of deep insertions; slow, sure and strong…

You are tiring.

I warn you not to move away if I untie your hands. You agree.

I get on to the table and kneel in front of you.

You stroke my balls. I start to masturbate, harder and harder. My body is rigid and starting to glow pink with effort.

I shoot into your face before we both target your mouth.

"Save some for me!" I plead.

I kiss you and you let some cum slake into my mouth. We kiss each other long and lingering.

We look at each other with deep, deep smiles.

I untie your legs.

You slap my face once; quite hard.

I turn on you, push you roughly to the bedroom, lay you down, lay down with you and hold you, just hold you.

We are at peace, you are satisfied with pain and I am shaking with pleasure.

Once the recovery is over, I need you to fuck my face.

Up on your knees, legs astride, pussy on my mouth, feeling the five-day growth. Your taste is divine. You love it.

"Fuck yourself!"

You start to masturbate, just above my mouth. I talk fucking filth to you. It gets you even hotter.

Suddenly, you spasm.

I pull your cunt right on to my mouth. I taste cum. I want it.

Now it's you who are quivering with pleasure.

You slump down on top of me.

My arms are wrapped round you.

You kiss my eyelids; first one then the other.

We both admit that "We are spent forces."

You turn. I cuddle into you and before we know it, morning has arrived.

10.

Mmmh, I am seriously horny after reading this porn! When will you get here? I promise you a streaming piss for minutes. I am getting excited thinking of the possibilities we can derive from the delightful toys you got from Amazon. Can you imagine?

Write me some more. I wish I could write like you. I will masturbate to that scene in the shower and the rough take on the table; hot! Not forgetting the sounds of you growling when pumping away. I can feel a wet spot on my panties! (I will cum hard, then go back to sleep.)

When do you leave for New York?

I love you, John.

My walking cunt!

I still can't believe that you are with me and want me; you a beautiful younger woman and me an older, ageing rocker – fucker. Never have I experienced total harmony of thought and desire in the pornographic world as I have with you. Other scenes? They end up being variations on the same basic tale but let's see. These ideas must come to mind; they cannot be forced.

You should give me an opening sentence idea then my mind can race into action; perhaps on how you would like to be 'taken'...

I definitely want to fuck you while someone is watching us – not touching us, not interfering in any way – just watching and probably ending with masturbation as we suck and fuck, suck and fuck each other's brains out.

John xxx

Why would you not believe that I am with you? Are you serious? I love every minute I am with you. You are a hot gentleman and I can never get enough of your attention and your dirty mind, of course! This cannot be bought.

The ideas have to flow, agreed. I forgot to comment about the Kenema incident in my yesterday's reply. I cannot remember the scene. I just wanted you to pick my cue and go with it. It had nothing to do with a premeditated scene. Like I told you, I have never been in a Dom position, so I ended up almost choking you and you getting upset about the whole setup. It's in your book. We have never talked about these things before. Maybe in passing but never giving it the attention it deserves. I want us to do that.

'We are at a small bistro that has low lights and candle light. We are sitting at the far end of the dining room across from each other, eyes twinkling with lusty secrets. I pass you my index finger to taste. You will take it in your mouth without question. It's when you realise it's wet, warm and full of pussy cum. You suck it hungrily, staring at me with dangerous looks. You give me those dark looks you get when you have a fully-fledged hard-on. My heart is racing fast, wondering what else I can do to shock you, to push you to do something without attracting the attention of other diners...' (continue).

I really like this exchanging of mails.

This is fantastic! At last, you are conveying the start of our journey. More importantly, each picture captures more than a thousand words of mine could ever do. Keep finding and sharing the pictures (where on earth do you see them anyway – keep it as your little secret, so that I can be constantly surprised).

The pictures were of various sado-masochistic poses, each of which Lorraine admitted that she would delight in experiencing...

When you read this, along with my other two messages, I shall be flying to New York. Time with my family and more time for healing WITH YOU!
Even if only a line or two, you'll get something from me each day. If you're in Addis, let me know so that I don't worry if I read nothing from you.
Love and more,
Your man in heat!

11.

'...we are at a small bistro that has low lights and candle lights, we are sitting at the far end of the dining room across each other, eyes twinkling with lusty secrets. I pass you my index finger to taste, you will take it in your mouth without question, it's when you realise it's wet, warm and full of pussy cum. You suck it hungrily, staring at me with dangerous looks, you give me those dark looks you get when you have a fully-fledged hard on, my heart racing fast, wondering what else I can do to shock you, to push you to do something without attracting the attention of other diners...'

I can't stand it. The waitress has been and gone. We are at a corner; a wall separates us from view. I really can't stand it. I drop to my knees and get under the table. You are not wearing panties or a G-string, like the walking cunt you are. I push your legs apart and ravage your secret parts with my tongue and mouth. You groan because you are fucking helpless with pleasure. I suck and fuck with my tongue, furiously; harshly even as my four-day-old beard starts to scratch your inner thighs. You grab the back of my hair, hard, pulling my face deeper into your cunt. I stay as long as I dare and as long as I can. I re-emerge. You are flushed and perspiring. I still can't stand it. I take you by the arm and march you through the restaurant. Our waitress sees us and wonders… We find the toilet. I place you on the cistern, with your feet on the toilet lid. Legs are pushed wide apart again. You cunt is glistening. I can't stop myself. My entire mouth embraces and consumes your clit, pussy and cunt, all in one sweep. I kiss and suck, kiss and suck. My cock is swollen. I let go of your cunt and quickly pull down my tight jeans. My cock stands erect. You look at it in disbelief. It looks even larger. I make sure you are balanced correctly. In I go. In I fuck. In I pump. We are going at it slowly and deeply. You see the door opening. I forgot to lock it in my haste to consume. It's the waitress. I don't care. She enters, locks the door, goes straight to my balls with her hand and with her other, takes your cheeks, moves towards your mouth and kisses you, wet, long and penetrating. She stays there as she strokes me further. I'm still pumping, giving you the hundred thrusts treatment but slowly. Your arms are now wrapped around me in both hunger and love. The waitress's hand moves away and replaces my balls with your breasts; one, then the other. You're almost delirious. She lets your face go with hand and mouth. She kisses me long, hard and deep. She reorganises herself, leaves and signals that we should lock the cubicle door. I do. We continue until there is no more.

"I love you, Lorraine, you cunt!"

"I love you, John, you fucking male whore; my fucking male whore and only mine!"

We disentangle, sort our clothes, kiss gently in conclusion, walk back to our discrete table. The meal continues. It's nice. The bill is brought. We pay and give the waitress a nice tip. We do not ask her name.

Hi, Baby!

I am sure you are in New York now. I hope the experience is better than you anticipated. Tell me how it is when you have time; no pressure.

Thank you so much for that delicious story, mmmh. One of these days, I will put myself to task and try my best to compose a sexy, cohesive story.

(I have just talked to Kate on the phone, I felt nauseous, seriously!)

Talk to me when you have time.

Sorry for this (unresolved issue that refuses to resolve).

What did you text Kate that Sunday? (Allow me please?) Remember when I said that I would like you to care how I feel about this? Make it easier for me.

WHAT? There was no text to Kate!

Thank you for spoiling my arrival in NY. I was so looking forward to reading messages from you and sending at least one, simply to acknowledge my arrival and growing love for you.

I arrived in the house twenty minutes ago.

Fuck! I can't believe it. Are you serious?

There was no fucking text to Kate 'that Sunday' or any other fucking day. This is just sick as well as being extremely unpleasant. Maintain this line of thought – in messages – and I will certainly go silent.

What? John, I am sorry. Seems like we are both raw. I was not trying to spoil your arrival. I am glad you arrived safely.

I was just reaching to my partner.

12.

It's three thirty a.m. The curse of jet lag! I miss you, Lorraine!

Oh, sweetie, I hope you finally succumbed to the much needed sleep. I miss you too, John (new for me, I do not do missing!). Rest some.

I'm so, so glad to have heard from you! I tried calling earlier (now there's no privacy). Even in these past eighteen hours, I have been concerned about so much, recognizing so much and feeling the importance of you so much! The only other thing I do miss are my children. The sense of family is more of an illusion; something I'm realizing in these eighteen hours!

I need you, Lorraine. I need you very much. My first openly declared claim on you is emotional: love! My second claim on you is fun: laughter. The last claim on you is sex: pornography and so much more.

I have a three hour drive later today, to collect my youngest. Another three hour drive back again.

Questions.

Are you going to Addis? If so, please let me know so that I can brace for prolonged silences.

Where will you be from 2nd January? At this moment, just a thought.

Finally, a broken agreement. I think I must open the toys package. It's wrapped in a silver wrapping with a customs declaration on top from China. I'll open it then wrap each item individually, in Christmas wrapping paper.

Love and more to my pornographic priestess!

Your man!

Hi, Baby!

Did you manage to catch some closed eye? I hope so.

I saw the 'private' call. I really don't pick up private number calls. If I knew it was you, of course I would have picked up.

Oh just thinking of you taking a long drive makes me miss you more. Don't feel bad about your kids; they are adults now. I guess you have to accept their new ways. It was inevitable, right? (But what do I know of such things.)

It's nice to know that you need me, I want you to need me, I love you, John. Don't take it lightly, I mean it.

I am still not sure about Addis. I just met with the new tailors and we have to start on my collection and I am broke and so many other reasons. I will definitely let you know if I do. About 2nd Jan? Are you kidding me? I would not make any arrangement until I knew what your schedule was like. I am yours until you change your mind.

Talk to me when you get back and when you have time.

Enjoy your family, sweetheart!

Love and tons of hugs!

Sweetheart!

By the time I get back, it'll be about two a.m. your time. NY is eight hours behind you. I have to make a number of calls and other arrangements. -Let me settle my mind. As to my heart? Fear not, young lady. I am yours till the day my time on this earth ends, in fun, love and so much more besides.

Your man xxx

I am all wrapped up in a body wrap (slapped some herbs and clay on my body then wrapped with cling-film). I feel like an Egyptian mummy. I was just chuckling to myself, thinking of you and what you would have done to me (I am not wearing any panties). I miss you.

Only got back a couple of hours ago... long round trip. Our youngest is back and bouncing around, literally.

There's a Kinky Card picture I saw some years ago, of a woman wrapped in cling-film; highly erotic and yes, you can imagine what I would do to you if I was there now and you had no panties on.... Or, you can tell me how you would like to be taken in that wrapped up state!

This 'missing you' business is serious! If there's something positive I can do about it, I shall.

Tomorrow, I drive to JFK to collect our daughter. Then all the usual family tensions will erupt, but that's family life.

I want to be with you, Lorraine, in love, fun and fucking gently and harshly. Those pictures you sent were *hot*. I keep looking at the pictures of you sent earlier then the latest erotic ones. I love them all and want more.

Love to my woman; my walking cunt!

My immensely loved Man!

I woke up this morning with an insatiable hunger for your cock! I was wet and my pussy was literally having a life of its own, oh my! I have cum to your face in my mind several times already! I am so horny, I might just fuck your dildo. I cannot get this need for your cock sated though. What will I do?

Mmmh, my love, I cannot wait for you to get back here. I will jump on you with a hunger for every inch of your beastly, beautiful, tasty body! I want to be with you too, John!

Thanks for the Kinky Cards, baby. I love them with your sweet messages. I will wrap myself in cling-film one evening and we can improvise how you would take me. Thinking of it is making feel very hot.

So, how do the toys look and feel like? Did you get turned on looking at them? Do you have ideas on how you would use them on me? (I betcha!)

I guess today is when you will have the full family together. Enjoy them all and write to me only when you have time and space. I totally understand and am so very happy for you!

I will try to find some more erotic pornographic material that will titillate your already titillated mind.

I love you.

Your pornographic priestess.

My immensely loved Man!

Gorgeous woman!

I woke up this morning with an insatiable hunger for your cock! ...what will I do?

Stick the dildo in dry, so that the friction – the slight discomfort of pain even – is heightened! Close your eyes and practice coming over my face and into my mouth.

Mmmh, my love, I cannot wait for you to get back here... I want to be with you too, John!

Let me confess something to you. I tried to change my flight today to return one week earlier because I need and hunger for you.

The fee was an extortionate sterling twelve hundred pounds! Very high season, so I abandoned that! Instead, there is no question on the matter; please meet me at the airport off the Brussels Airways flight on Friday 9th. Get a taxi driver you trust. I shall, of course, pay the round trip. You take me straight home to your place. We end up in bed. Having flown straight from New York (almost twenty-four hours, including airport hanging around time. I shall be tired but whatever else happens, I shall need to stick my tongue then my cock deep into your cunt!)

Thanks for the Kinky Cards, baby...

This is a certainty. In fact, I shall wrap you in cling film but keep your breasts exposed so that nipple clamps can be attached.

So, how do the toys look and feel like?

I removed the outer wrapping. Saw all, but kept the clear package in place. I then wrapped the entire thing in Christmas paper. We shall both unpack and explore. The whip looks inviting.

I will try to find some more erotic pornographic material that will titillate your already titillated mind.

Frankly, I can't get enough of it and your associated thoughts. So delicious, so fucking delicious, you slutty cunt!

I love you.

And I love you in all things, boiling down to being your male whore.

Your pornographic priestess.

Yes, yes, yes!

Now, for compensation for us both because of my failure to return to you sooner: please choose somewhere for us to go for the weekend of 16th to 18th. I don't mind where. I just want us free of all trappings; just being able to dress up to eat and to show each other off accordingly.

You are a fantastic woman, Lorraine. -This time apart is overwhelmingly healing and, therefore, so important to us both.

Love and more to my walking cunt!

My love!

Reading from you has become an addiction (does one week only count?). It's a pleasure.

I have been talking to Alice the whole evening; she is somewhat down and I was there. She has gone to bed now and I am in mine, horny and mildly frustrated with this much want for you!

Oh baby! I was hoping you will be here by the 2nd of January! Oh bloody hell, I have no choice but to wait. Don't freak out so much if I attack you in the cab! The thought counts though (that you almost changed your ticket for me). You get an extra blowjob, the morning after your arrival, for being super sweet and loving.

I will be at the airport on time (of course!). Just send me your time of arrival when you get your itinerary.

I will find a place for our getaway. It has to compensate for that horror place and should sooth away whatever ugliness we have gone through. This should be beautiful. It has to be.

Meanwhile, enjoy these few photos. Tell me if you can see them with my eyes. Tell me what you think.

Love and more to my fantastic male whore!

My love!
Reading from you has become an addiction (does one week only count?)
It's a pleasure.

That's the whole point. You become an addiction. I can't get enough of you, in words and shared pictures. It is also part of the healing process...

Oh, baby! I was hoping you will be here by the 2nd of January... don't freak out so much if I attack you in the cab!

You are most welcome in the cab. You can unbutton me, take out my cock and give me a blow job after we've cleared the pay barrier...

.

I will find a place for our getaway. It has to compensate for that horror place...

It has to be. Lorraine! This is essential, even if it turns out to be purely emotional; staring into each other's eyes, touching, hand-holding, caressing and sleeping. I want the weekend to end with us believing in each other completely and without fear, knowing that we are everything to each other that a man and woman can ever be, in the worlds, and I mean worlds that we inhabit, whether pure or disgusting. Both are crucial to our combination; our commitment to each other.

The cling film pictures induce an urge for me to piss on them. You want to rub your naked body against each one, masturbating and begging me to push gently but firmly into your asshole with my cock as you do so (are you proud of yourself for letting me fuck your ass – you should be!).

The cunt pictures demand our joint attention. You want to suck them, each separately, before you take my cock and force me to fuck one then the other.

The rear view of that black beauty sees you demanding the strap-on and you fucking her, while my cock is in her mouth, with our lips (yours and mine) colliding in lots of wet kisses and mutual spitting - with hunger and passion. Once you've induced her orgasm, I fuck your cunt while she lavishes her kisses on your breasts and mouth; your tongues entwined – so fucking hot!

I want you to understand that in this context, I shall do anything for you and with you. I have found what I hope to be the total partner in love, laughter and pornography, my high priestess in the genre. You are all women to me!

Good morning, my love!

I am glad you appreciated the photos. I still cannot believe how easily it is to share these things with you. I have always felt guilty, embarrassed even before. Thanks for being you, John. Because of you, I am more confident about my sexual curiosities.

Do the same for me. Let me in. Let me know what your hidden fantasies are all about, uncensored.

Yes! I am proud that I let you stick your huge cock in my ass. It was surprisingly not so painful (until the next day). I want you to fuck all my holes and I will fuck yours too.

I surrender to you, my great male whore! (Only mine!)

Heading to Kate's for her daughter's birthday (wish I didn't have to). I don't plan to be there for long, so I hope I can catch up with you later, my Lovely Man!

Your pornographic princess.

Good morning, my love!
I am glad you appreciated the photos... I am more confident about my sexual curiosities.

This is awful that you should have choked off your desire to express such desire, no hesitation to share. I am you man – your partner – to share with.

Let me know what your hidden fantasies are all about, uncensored!

As you know, I tend to follow, to react, rather than lead but have you ever thought about selling my sexual services for our profit?

Yes! I am proud that I let you stick your huge cock in my ass.

This is beautiful and shall be done to us both by us both!

I surrender to you, my great male whore! (only mine!)

And I to you, my angel slut!

Just got home and hungrily went for the mail, you hottie. Be ready for body damage. I crave for you, and... and in love, LOVE!

I await your mail... (Abba in the background.)

Why do you want me? (Two thousand words.)

You should be with me now. Love is an understatement.

Have fun.

13.

'Why do you want me? You should be with me now.'

Beautiful Lorraine!
You are telepathic! I have been thinking about these things all day and indeed every day since I left Freetown but today, things became more pronounced and that is why I told you earlier that I was going to write to you later... after all others were in bed. I should be with you now. I wanted to be with you much sooner but life's practicalities intervened. Yet the enforced absence is proving to be a godsend.

Love is indeed an understatement. This is what I am wrestling with now. I know what is going on and I both welcome and fear it. The bottom line though is that it is a wonderful – a thrilling – feeling; one of elation even. You have done something to me. You are doing something to me. That 'something' is what I am trying to understand. Under normal circumstances, after what we had been through and the evening I walked away, that should have been the end of things. You even admitted as much 'you would not bother me again' (paraphrasing). Then, you were moved to communicate again and again and again. The love (and passion) you had – and you still have – even after everything, poured on to the pages and into me. I read and re-read, astounded by you and your determination to convey your feelings as well as your fears. What I thought I had closed on was clearly not so. You reopened all my latent passion and desire for you; love was simply sleeping, waiting to be woken...

Then you ask, 'why do I want you?' This is the other part of the telepathy. I have been thinking about this all day. Why indeed? The answers are clear to me. (1) We understand each other but why do I want you? Because you understand me! (2) We have the same humour. (3) We understand the pain and ecstasy of love. (4) You are a gorgeous-looking woman. (5) I adore the thought and reality of falling asleep with you and waking up with you. (6) You're a terrific fuck, in all genres; emotional and pornographic. (7) You do not judge me with my wild thoughts. (8) You want me to lust for you. (9) Finally, 'why do I want you?' I'm in love with you!

Now I must sleep. xxx

I just came to your mail, my greatest love! I will write to you in a little bit, I cannot help it any more, Let me hear your voice. I do not think I have ever had these feelings before, (exhilarating in a scary way, I am not in control any more).

Oh, John, you are the one!

...in a bit!

Had to let you know. I just had a very thrilling orgasm with no prompt from me in any form! I am losing it! Sloppy sucks and kisses all over your lovely body! I finally understand what 'passionate' means, for the first time my 'still' unfulfilled life.

I can ever express enough of my feelings, intense, mind blowing feelings I have for you now. You fucking male whore! You are mine!

Beautiful creature! I'm just up! People around! All this tirade of love and sex is phenomenal... More later from you and then me.

My hot man!

Sorry for my loving rants in my earlier mails, I am just so aware of my feelings for you and my frustration is quite evident from my rants. Come home sooner or you will find a chicca with a missing cunt (from too much rubbing at your memory).

Your walking cunt.

Wouldn't that be beautiful – just a random thought – to share together; our mouths hungrily sharing another tasty cunt's juices? (Am I tiring you with my lusty thoughts of us?) I am so hungry for you!

First, we could do wonderfully wicked things to her; you and I. Secondly, how can I fucking get tired of this, so fucking beautifully hot, you slut cunt, you gorgeous creature and my woman in all things!

The cling film pictures induce an urge for me to piss on them. You want to rub your naked body against each one, masturbating and begging me to push gently but firmly into your asshole with my cock as you do so. (Again, are you proud of yourself for letting me fuck your ass? You should be!).

The cunt pictures demand our joint attention. You want to suck them; each separately before you take my cock and force me to fuck one then the other.

The rear view of that black beauty sees you demanding the strap-on and you fucking her, while my cock is in her mouth, with our lips (yours and mine) colliding in lots of wet kisses and mutual spitting with hunger and passion. Once you've induced her orgasm, I fuck your cunt while she lavishes her kisses on your breasts and mouth; your tongues entwined, so fucking hot!

I want you to understand that in this context, I shall do anything for you and with you. I have found what I hope to be the total partner in love, laughter and pornography, my high priestess in the genre. You are all women to me.

Pleasure! Absolutely! I love you so much, John.

(Picture of Ethiopian beauty)
...I licked her pussy, she would stick her finger in me when her French husband was busy talking to customers at their pub. She used to freak me out but it was fun. Talk to me!

She looks hot! I'm calling you in two minutes!

Where are you?

That's the best phone call I have ever received; your voice is intoxicating!

Sweetheart! I was speaking from the garage in NY (it was freezing but the only place where none of the three children could hear me).

Keep thinking about this enforced separation and in reality, how it is helping us both to understand all aspects of each other. We shall benefit from this when we come together again...

Love and porn' to my woman!

Are you punishing me? (I gladly take it!) But I want more of your sexy voice.

Okay, I just read the last mail. I do understand. I am appreciating this separation a lot. I love you.

You SHALL be punished! Define the punishments you want. My voice again tomorrow, if I can get some privacy. Remember; in so much, you lead and I follow... so you define.

Agreed and understood, my one and only male whore!

This is all a solid foundation. Recognise and bask in the prospect of so much to come that is good between us love and hardcore porn... Finally for now (off to make lunch for three children) – define at least two forms of punishment that I am to administer. Be explicit so that I can be put in (even more) heat when I return to Gmail later today. You're a fantastic woman, Lorraine, a terrific slut and the best whore ever... which is slightly unjust because I have never been aware of being with a whore. So, you are the epitome of 'the oldest game in town'. I am sure no other can come close to you in beauty, sensuality and skills, with hands, tongue and pussy.

Fuck my face, you cunt. My unshaved face is now four days old – the way you like it – a bit rough for your cunt.

I will reply to this mail when I have thought it through, like a good whore that I am. I am about to start my ritual. I have a bad case of insomnia coupled with very lusty thoughts of my newly gained man whore. You could not get here sooner?

Oh, my ritual being having your rough face between my legs, my pussy dripping, quivering, knowing what's coming next. Your gorgeous long tongue suddenly sweeps from my tight asshole to my already hot dripping cunt. A shot of power runs through my entire system, my cunt does not want to part from your mouth; it's so delicious, rough and lovingly so. I want to fuck your face. I want to love your face with my cunt's wetness. I rub your face with my plump fully engorged clit, moist droplets of sweet cunt juices dripping on your face, then...

I surprise you. I take you by your fully erect monster cock. I lick all the savoured pre-cum that has been generously pouring out. I gently tug you to the bathroom stall. I direct you to the shower, me astride you, my bladder full, ready to burst. I finally give you the golden shower that you have been wishing for. I piss on your face and mouth, streams and streams of hot piss just showering you with love.

Take the cue.

Your very obedient whore.

Sorry, I mixed the ritual with the erotic fantasy. My ritual is to read porn to the closest story that resembles us as possible, while masturbating, and it does not take long for me to cum... but I am still left with a void that can only be filled with your physical self.

My god, Lorraine! This is stunning stuff. The pictures are truly fantastic! You look even more beautiful and even hotter than when I left you... and you looked hot (and tortured, though not pleasantly) then. I can't get enough of you or your unbelievable pictures.

I still wait for your two punishment scenarios – it is you to be punished, as you, yourself, requested, so let me know.

I will think hard about the two punishment scenarios and will get back to you, but tomorrow. Tell me what you thought about me pissing on your face.

You asked me to continue the story and I shall... but the pissing scene must, absolutely must, be implemented. You must do it. You must pour it over my face and if I do not open my mouth, you must hold my nose so that it is forced open. You must then pour your piss right down my throat. I must swallow. When tasting your cunt sometimes, soon after your toilet, I have tasted the residual dribble, like weak whisky, which I've told you before.

When I shower each morning, I stick my finger deep into my asshole and pretend it's your finger. I push it right in. Sometimes there is just a hint of shit, a drop, on the edge of my finger. I wash it clean immediately, then push my finger in again, imagining it to be yours again, then withdraw it and look with pride when it is completely clean and therefore ready for your fingers and your tongue.

My love, in this frenzied atmosphere (you and me) I wish I could just abandon everything and come to you but of course, I will not. As you know now, the fee to come one week earlier was extortionate. That money can be used for other things (like a couple of our weekend escapes).

Again, the pictures are fantastic and your breasts and nipples are ripe for being attacked.

As for the paid male whore thing; a woman older than you, not particularly attractive, just frustrated and in need of release. You must arrange and you must be present the entire time, or any variation on the theme. Just a wicked thought. You define, my Lorraine! You define...

I am YOUR man and you are MY woman.

John xxx

Baby, I like it when I stick my tongue deep into your asshole, like the smooth tight assrim; the outside, make it wet with my wet mouth, shoving my tongue deep into you and you backing against my face, loving it that you moan, calling me a whore.

I will piss on you, I am ready to try that fantasy out and for sure it will be beautiful as you paint it or even more.

These ripe titties of mine are yours to attack! Anytime!

14.

John decided to compose a mutually supporting declaration, something to give them emotional solidity. His to Lorraine was...

To me, Lorraine, this is the epitome of wickedness! It is delicious in its duality of symbolism, good and wicked (which means even better). In a curious way, it captures you and me. This is the beginning of the extremes we both seek to explore with each other's help, care and love. I love you to the point of madness; a good madness, a creative madness but one where I am willing to let myself go and lay myself and my heart at the mercy of one Lorraine Cooper. Do you understand this? I am saying to you what you are increasingly saying to me. You want the totality of me and my welcome of you, in all your sublime, erotic, sensual and pornographic ambitions. Let me tell you that, in such matters (and more besides), you have found the ideal partner. How do I know? Because we have come through fire to get to this point. When I finally get back to you, all the necessary healing will be behind us. We shall recombine with a month of reconstruction 'in the bag'. Love and porn, your man.

He interpreted hers to him...

I PROMISE to take care of you. I am letting myself go and trusting you to always be there, no walking out on each other, no threats, no disrespect for each other, to always listen and empathize, sympathize, be patient... I promise to work on my weak points and harder on being your pornographic priestess. Reading your sentiments about your feelings about me makes me feel very grateful, special and beautiful; thank you, my whore. You have the totality of me. We will be fine. I believe that. I cannot wait to have you back, back in my life and bed. I have found my perfect man, let's be good to each other.

This was signed directly and vicariously as follows:

I regard this as a written declaration of love and devotion, let alone an emotional contract between us. freely given and freely exchanged.

Consider my signature appended:

John Evans, 22nd December, 2014.

I shall consider your signature also appended:

Lorraine Cooper, 23rd December, 2014.

You are my man, no doubt about that!

They took the logical step and explored their boundaries further in this perfect erotic relationship.

Thank you for the erotic card. Hot! Yes! I see that in us, I would like us to have a sit down, coffee and tea in a quiet cafe and have the conversations about boundaries and anything else, but we can still write to each other but I doubt if we will have many boundaries. We are both very kinky.

What are your boundaries? I can't think of any except perhaps:

1. I won't pimp you for money.

2. I won't do a threesome with another man (selfish maybe but I just can't do it).

3. I won't watch you being fucked by another man.

What are yours? (But don't answer now, unless it's easy.) Leave it till tomorrow or, in your case, later today. Meanwhile, I have a longer letter drafted. I shall send it much later so that you can have something to welcome you when you wake up.

My return, when it comes, may be anti-climactic. We must be calm and patient with each other. The idea of quiet coffee and tea and talking would be good, on Saturday (after being together on Friday night on arrival) and after my grocery shopping for the next few days.

I am alone with my boy. It's six fifteen and I must make his meal (and mine). I shall go through all the pictures you have sent me again later. They are delicious! You are delicious! The equilibrium we are developing – the balance of understanding between you and me, me and you – must be nurtured and cared for as we seek to nurture and care for each other.

Meanwhile, I hope my suggested boundaries have not offended or disappointed you, my dearest love.

Love to Lorraine!

John xxx'

This is very easy for me!
1. I would never be pimped out.

2. I have never desired to be with more than one man.

3. I can never be fucked by another man while you watched.

I've just returned from shopping, to be greeted by your two messages. Thank you! Let me embed my reactions to the first now. Then I shall read the second.

1. I would never be pimped out? *Thank you!*

2. I have never desired to be with more than one man? *Thank you again!*

3. I can never be fucked by another man while you watched!? *And finally, thank you ultimately. You are mine alone. My cock is yours and yours alone. xxx*

Then John read her boundaries.

1. Health safety at all times when and if we indulge in a threesome, you cannot finger her and finger me with the same hand. This is one of my greatest fears. Understood and agreed.

2. We are not to pick prostitutes, friends or anyone familiar to us. Understood and agreed.

3. You cannot exchange numbers or anything personal with any of the girls. Understood and agreed.

4. The girl/s cannot ever sleep over! When done, a cab should be arranged for her/them. Understood and agreed.

5. *I am not always in a mood for a threesome and would appreciate if John understood that.* My love, my first hunger is for you. Anything else is secondary. I would appreciate if Lorraine understood that.

6. *I would prefer if we never had girls in either our homes.* That is best; agreed.

He called her.

Thank you for the phone call, I am blushing like a teenager; your voice and words are always appreciated.

Let me get back to my letter. I hope everything is well at your home. Phone calls are so difficult anyway and twice as bad when neither can hear the other properly.

Write my love and more pictures if you are in the mood to take and send. They (and you) are delicious!

She sent him three hot pictures of her sexy self.

You're driving me crazy, my beauty. If you feel you can, a picture or two of your wet, glistening pussy cunt... Meanwhile, thank you for the erotic card!

To me, Lorraine, this is the epitome of wickedness! It is delicious in its duality of symbolism; good and wicked (which means even better). In a curious way, it captures you and me. This is the beginning of the extremes we both seek to explore with each other's help, care and love. I love you to the point of madness. A good madness, a creative madness but one where I am willing to let myself go and lay myself and my heart at the mercy of one, Lorraine. Do you understand this? I am saying to you what you are increasingly saying to me. You want the totality of me and my welcome of you, in all your sublime, erotic, sensual and pornographic ambitions. Let me tell you that, in such matters (and more besides), you have found the ideal partner. How do I know? Because we have come through fire to get to this point. When I finally get back to you, all the necessary healing will be behind us. We shall recombine with a month of reconstruction 'in the bag'! Love and porn, Your man whore!

I promise to take care of you.

I am letting myself go and trusting you to always be there. No walking out on each other, no threats, no disrespect for each other; to always listen and empathize, sympathise, be patient...

I promise to work on my weak points and harder on being your pornographic priestess.

Reading your sentiments about your feelings about me makes me feel very grateful, special and beautiful. Thank you, my whore. You have the totality of me.

We will be fine, I believe that, I cannot wait to have you back, back in my life and bed. I have found my perfect man. Let's be good to each other.

15.

First, let me just confess to being overwhelmed by the pictures you have sent today (yesterday for you). They really are 'out of-this-world'! They capture the erotic spirit and sensual essence of you. Apart from just enjoying them as a man, I deeply appreciate why you did them and sent them. They convey not only your pleasure in yourself but your deep commitment to me and us. Thank you so, so much! I have just looked at them again (and again), along with all the other pictures sent. Words fail me. In this regard, you are *Perfection*!

Baby, let me embed immediate reactions to your erotic and deeply emotional tirade (consolidated below). It will then be followed by a more considered reply, full of fucking and dreams.

1. I just came to your mail, my greatest love! I will write to you in a little bit, I cannot help it any more, Let me hear your voice. I do not think I have ever had these feelings before (exhilarating in a scary way; I am not in control any more). I think I understand and believe this.

Oh, John, you are the one! ...and that is what is wonderfully scary. The more I read from you, I realise that 'at last',

128

I have found the true partner in all our desires; love and erotic truth.
I expand on this later.

2. *Listen: 'you are my treasure.' You are!* As you
are mine, Lorraine!

3. *(had to let you know) I just had a very
thrilling orgasm with no prompt from me in any
form! I am losing it! Sloppy sucks and kisses all
over your lovely body! I finally understand what
'passionate' means, for the first time my 'still'
unfulfilled life –* this will be part of my reflective text, below.

4. *I can never express enough of my feelings;
intense, mind blowing feelings that I have for
you now! You fucking male whore!* Yes! You are
mine! Yes and keep me!

5. *I know why I cannot sate myself (wet moist
dripping pussy, so moist, it's literally puffing
silent puffs out...* I want to taste and inhale these puffs...

6. *Oh, jeez! Please tolerate my hushed
emotional (dimwit fever) horniness for you!
Can you let me?* Are you kidding? This is just the start!
Tolerate? I yearn for this again and again and again; with so much
more wanted and needed from you...

7. *(from the second mail) I love you so much!
You are my peer. (Does that make sense to you?)
I understand and appreciate you.* This is the final
piece of this particular emotional jigsaw. My responses and
interpretations shall follow in normal text xxx

My slut, my walking cunt! There are four key phrases offered in your emotional and erotic outbursts. Let me highlight them:

1. 'Oh, John, you are the one'.
2. 'I finally understand what 'passionate' means, for the first time my 'still' unfulfilled life'.
3. 'Please tolerate my hushed emotional (dimwit fever) horniness for you'.
4. '...you are my peer.'

I have been labouring under an illusion. I have assumed that you have enjoyed such fucking and expressions of passion since you woke up to your particular form of, at times, beautifully twisted, sexual and pornographic experiences. I have assumed that you have been able to express your thoughts and dreams with whichever partner you have been with. I have assumed that you have had a free-flowing adult partnership of enjoying and practicing these ideas, in comfort and with confidence because of the person you have been with at the time. Then I start to recognise that my illusion – my assumption – about you is wrong; entirely misplaced. It becomes clearer when I consolidate your fucking tirade above.

'Oh, John, you are the one'. It's as if you have been searching (and experiencing) but have never found the total package of emotion and porn in one man. Now you have and you are in disbelief. My own elation in this fact is that I share the same thoughts but at least I have been able to give vent to them in writing, whether in dreams or in faltering reality. Now you have me and you can start to recognize that we have only touched the

surface, that there is so much more that you recognize – I hope – that you tend to be the initiator – the dreamer – and that I react or follow... but not always! Sometimes your man will just seize the moment...

'I finally understand what 'passionate' means, for the first time my 'still' unfulfilled life'. This, to me, is a sadness; that you have experienced the erotic but are telling me that the pure passion has been absent. That's not good and must be attended to, in both words and deeds. You *are* my passion and I *am* yours. Let yourself go. Let it rip – and at times, when I sense that you really do want to be ripped apart, I shall oblige with great force and that (for far too long with you) missing word, passion.

'Please tolerate my hushed emotional (dimwit fever) horniness for you'. Are you kidding me? Tolerate? What I will not tolerate is if you do NOT share and express your horniness for me in all its pornographic guises. I want this and I want so much more in that realm of both dreams and reality. You're my woman, Lorraine, and I am going to treat you in that totality of the meaning 'my woman'. This means all things: loved, fucked, used, abused, taken gently, taken with force, spat upon, sworn at, pissed upon on your face and into your mouth, treated like an angel, like a slut and a whore; my whore, my personal sex machine and so much more that is within you and waiting to be expressed by you, for you and to me!

'...you are my PEER'. In fact, there is more to this simple phrase than the phrase itself. It conveys a complete belief in me as a friend in all manner of things but at this moment, of learning and experiencing all matters of fucking – your hands, your mouth, your asshole and your cunt. The underlying theme in all this is that you have never felt able to express freely in all matters concerning your

straight (emotional) and twisted (beautifully pornographic) desires. If I am right, then welcome to the new world of John and Lorraine... or Lorraine and John!

Love and porn to my delicious woman!

Your man!

P.S. As for my return, permit me to plan a little. It offers structure. I shall arrive and we shall go straight home to your place. We shall engage in each other's pleasure, to include the unwrapping of one gift (the toys we can unwrap anytime). We shall end up in bed, close, emotional and passionate. Eventually, we shall sleep. The following day, we shall emerge, get coffee and tea, get out, get breakfast, get groceries, get my things and let me get to Bintumani to unpack. We shall then resume together at your place, go to a nice quiet restaurant together, eat together, talk together, look into each other's eyes together, whisper love and devotion together, return to your place together, embrace together and let the stars move us as they think fit. After lunch on Sunday, I shall get back to Bintumani and prepare myself for Monday morning's first day back at work. What follows, we shall decide together, in partnership.

I have woken up to the most wonderful read. Thank you. Give me a bit of time to digest, enjoy and will slowly compose a long letter to you. Thank you for drafting the declaration of love. I will save mine, to remind me of our pact, to love and to protect.

I love you, John Evans.

I look forward to the 'long letter' but only after a good digestion on your part. On this letter, my angel, all you have to confirm is whether my basic understanding of you is correct; 25%, 50%, 75% or 100%. If less than full understanding, give me the score and tell me where I have faltered in my interpretation...

I am sorry, I forgot to answer to this letter. Yup! You got it and me, perfectly. I really get surprised with you at times; good surprises, of how you are able understand me on deeper levels, but I should not be surprised. I first understood - or realized - that from reading your books. You have a deep understanding of human beings and I am a lucky girl! 100% perfect. Thank you!

My baby. I'm going to respond to your kind reply a little more, much later tonight, because an additional level of interpretation has just occurred to me. You'll read it tomorrow. It won't be that long but it will be central to our combined being.

Meanwhile (and again), your pictures are sizzling in heat and pure, unadulterated sexual passion and hunger. I am your partner in this and all that remains to be uncovered and discovered, within you, within me and between us. Thank you, Thank You and THANK YOU, gorgeous, lovely and ultimately believing (in us) Lorraine!

16.

Books. Can I have my books back now? I need to read them again with appreciation, rather than with blind anger; they are fantastic reads! Please.

Are you sure and which ones? I really don't want to trigger all that badness again!

I am sure, it was just so new for me. I am great, I promise. I want to appreciate them.

Lorraine! This scares me... because it is what started the whole mess; the whole mistrust; the whole 'manipulation' accusation. Anyway, all the hard copies are in England, hidden; not in NY, where I have no place to hide anything!

Okay, no worries, you will share again when I have proven to you that there's nothing to be scared about. No worries, my love.

Thank you, Lorraine! I appreciate that very much!

Hugs and wet kisses!

This remained a perpetual undercurrent in their relationship. He had shared his first book with her, thinking it might trigger not only empathy but also, a recognition that the book was entirely fiction. That is to say 'yes', it was an exploration of emotion, then desire, then aspects of an almost innocent pornography – if indeed, there is such a thing.

When first read, she went into a tirade; a frenzy. That she was being manipulated, used, treated as an experiment. What John tried to reveal to her was that any cyber-relationship, or even a real-live one, would go through the same basic stages. What he tried to persuade her was that any experience he had previously was all part of the journey, trying to find that total woman in all respects. The fact that he had not found her till now was testament to all the previous failure; that he had arrived at her feet (at times, literally), as the next attempt to find that elusive quality in a woman: love, sex, sensuality, eroticism, pornography and a willingness to explore that collective, alternative lifestyle.

When Lorraine was lucid and therefore balanced in her mind, John could almost believe that she would treat the book (actually the books – all seven of them) as a 'fantastic read'. The 'almost' was important. John considered himself a 'student of the human condition' and in particular, the 'man-woman' stuff. After all, his books were about that stuff, particularly his own emotional (and at times, sensual) travails; his journey through that minefield for which others seemed to walk through unhindered – no explosions but in his case, not so lucky. If only he could get her to see each book (and each sensual, erotic and even pornographic description), as a yearning for what he considered to be unobtainable (after, now, seventeen years of writing and, therefore, seventeen years of exploring).

He admitted to himself early in this journey that he was attempting to enrich his sagging marriage (hoping that the excitement of this parallel world would spill over to the domestic realities), It didn't quite work out that way but it certainly helped retain his morale. It also triggered a rich vein of writing (totally unprofitable as it transpired; being reduced to the self-publishing mode); with, at least, a measure of satisfaction.

If only Lorraine could understand this wider picture of the 'journey of emotional and erotic exploration'. If only she could understand if a previous encounter had been successful, he would not be with her now. There was the irony. John's failures had led him to Lorraine. The question then was. 'could she see that'? If only she could. If only!

17.

Pussy. I could not take a better photo; lighting is poor for pussy shots, I suppose.

You kept you panties / G-string on. It heightens the pussy lips. Mmmmm!

Next time you feel inclined, no panties and legs and therefore pussy, wide open and if yet another, showing the dildo inserted.

I will try that during the day, when no one is around, for you, my perfect man.

My god! I commented while still looking at the attachment. In full picture view, it looks so real, so edible, touchable, kissable and suckable; beautiful!

Masturbate your cock to my photo; I am definitely going to cum to yours.

That has to be done late at night and unlike you – who uses masturbation as various forms of delight and release – I find doing so alone (even if, for you, thousands of miles away), sad. Let's see what I might be able to muster for you. If I succeed, I shall drink all the cum in honour of you!

There's nothing sad about masturbating, baby! Take a photo of your cum, I am trembling with delight at the thought of you drinking your cum; that thought always has me wet. Am I perverted?

Are you perverted? In this, you are perfect, *Perfection*, a joy, everything I have always wanted in a woman; a real woman and you are precisely that and all mine!

Don't you understand the beauty of perversion between consenting adults?

I really do yearn for these extra pictures, if you can manage it. If not, we'll do so when I am with your again, with glistering juices included and / or with you pulling your pussy lips apart so that I (and the camera) can see right in.

We will do the photos together.

Terrific, you lovely woman!

She then sent five hot pictures, including one of her breasts, succulent and worthy of being sucked, caressed and sometimes squeezed with harshness, at her request and to her subsequent pleasure.

You are truly fucking delicious, my woman. I still cannot believe that you want me in my entirety and yet I am so, so glad and so, so grateful that you have chosen to persevere and then bestow all your love, beauty, and pornographic delights upon me. We are going to be wonderful together. I have searched for you for such a long time! Thank you, my walking slut-cunt, my delicious woman, my Lorraine xxx

Just looked at your pictures again. Your body is to kill for. Your breasts are to die for. Your face – that delicious and fuckable face – it is to be kissed, pissed upon, slapped and spat upon, before cumming all over it, rubbing it in and licking it off, letting the residue on my tongue be consumed by your mouth and tongue...

No person has showered me so much praise and love as you have. I want to love you with my all! I miss your growling voice in my ear when you are fucking me hard from being, when you are calling me fucking whore... mmmhh, fucking me from behind.

This is an additional side of that long letter. I cannot believe, either, that you have never been showered with praise and love in the way that I do. I do so because it is a natural consequence of your beauty and sensual hunger. As for my growling voice as I am fucking my whore, there's lots of that to come (with rape and being torn apart, included), my walking slut!

Mmmmh, I await to be raped by my man.

I shall oblige, sometimes, with slow, threatening verbal deliberations and at others, fast and furious! Every time I think of you, I calculate your time of day and how you are.

9th January, 2015 seems so far away! I welcome any abuse from you to my body. I crave it because it's you. I uploaded the 'Living Earth' app the same day you left for England, so I can check your time and to remember that there's an eight hour difference. I am at home most of the time, trying to read with obsessive delicious thoughts of you swimming through my mind, constantly!

My baby! Listen (i.e. read this) carefully! The time apart has been so important to us up to this point. The healing has been immense and is still in process. The little wobble about my books attests to the need to clear away all the residual fears. For that, time, love exchanges, pornographic dreams and their translation into an eventual reality, takes a little while longer.

I leave in the evening of Thursday 8th January and arrive in the evening of 9th January – scheduled to get in at 21.55. In the bad old days, I would have insisted on not being met; going straight to Bintumani, sleeping, waking, doing my shopping then coming to you. Now, in the good new days, none of that! I want you so badly at the airport. I have already sent you the weekend 'plan'. It shall be done. There will be bed, sleep, fucking, fun and talking quietly on Saturday evening.

The one thing you must understand is that the closest I have come to feeling this way with anyone was five years ago and as I told you time and again, I never, repeat never felt safe. I even went to therapy because of it, at her suggestion and introduction – pathetic, in my opinion.

What I want to feel with you, apart from all our delicious dreams and aspirations, is safe, completely safe, absolutely safe. That I will never have any fear of you straying from me, enjoying others more than me. I want you to feel that you can flourish socially but that I can know that I am, even then, totally and completely yours and that you are totally and completely mine. Please, Lorraine, let me feel completely safe and protected in your love, desire, in your arms and in bed. This is an absolute requirement beyond all else!

John xxx

Embedded.

For that, time, love exchanges, pornographic dreams and their translation into an eventual reality, takes a little while longer.

AGREED, Sweetheart, I appreciate what we have come through, I appreciate this time apart and I don't want us to rush through things (that's what we did after meeting). I will not pressure you about the books, I can wait until we are both comfortable.

There will be bed, sleep, fucking, fun and talking quietly on Saturday evening. *I shall be at the airport to receive you into my arms, my bed and in my life!*

I never, repeat never felt safe! I even went to brief therapy because of it – pathetic in my opinion. *We share the same fears, sometimes I think me more than you, you have to understand one thing, that I will not take being cheated on. That would literally break me. I will not cheat on you!*

Please, Lorraine, let me feel completely safe and protected in your love, desire, in your arms and in bed. This is an absolute requirement beyond all else. *My sweet love, I have no ambitions to enjoy any other person other than with you, I have never even hinted that I am like that. I promised to be your protector and I will abide by that. I am your Lorraine, in all totality. I will show you! Sweetheart, I am asking the same from you, I have to feel utterly safe. I cannot have suspicions (I will not look for them). I want to always feel like I am the only one. I mean, it's very important for me; no ex-girlfriends calling you or texting. Totally mine and me, yours!*

Please, baby, be careful! Your ex-boyfriends are in touch with you... and you them.

I was talking to my ex, which I never tried to hide from you. I have not spoken to him in a while and I promise to cut all communication. I am not talking to any other man.

142

My baby, see how sensitive we both still are! All I know is that I want to be absolutely and totally yours in all things and for you to be mine, absolutely mine in all things. This we can do, my love. I know we can. I just want you to possess me completely and for me to possess you completely. Do you believe we can reach this state of ecstasy, because I do!

We are! We both want to possess each other; we should. I want you, John. You are everything and enough for me. With patience, love and devotion, baby, we are going to be just wonderful.

Agreed, you delicious creature! Now rest, while I start cooking for the family. More from me later tonight, for you to wake up to. Love and passion to my fucking Lorraine.

Okay, my baby, I will watch a movie and maybe sleep halfway through it. Thank you for being you. Enjoy your family and dinner. Goodnight, my pornographic beast!
I love you.

I am loving you more and more. Feel embraced by that thought with pure and filthy thoughts combined. I feel elated with your love and presence in my life. Stay in it! Stay with me! Sleep well when sleep descends.

143

18.

I want to be the source of your release, your sexual and emotional release...

You may punish me.

1. I will give you my mouth and throat to use and abuse with your giant cock.

2. I will become your urinal when you get home.

3. I will consume copious amount of water so that I can give you streams and streams of piss whenever you demand it.

4. My arse-hole will be cleaned and ready for your mouth.

5. I will lick your arse-hole clean and I will fuck you with a dildo to your satisfaction.

6. You can slap, spit, bite, pinch and choke me because I am a whore and whores need to be punished.

7. I will not greedily swallow all the cum but remember to share some with you.

8. I shall not protest if you choose to fuck my pussy and a dildo in my ass at the same time.

9. I will gladly agree to be blindfolded, collared, spanked, whipped and abused for your contented pleasure.

10. I will answer to piss, slut, whore, cunt, bitch names.

I tried to compose a letter but it was not coming together beautifully and so I decided to send you a list (a bucket list) instead. You can add more scenarios.

Your walking cunt!

Xxx

John was more than just astonished at this declaration of desire from Lorraine. It was, to him, an astounding revelation of submissive intent and degradation – all for her pleasure but knowing her, to assign such pleasure to the person inflicting the punishment. It hadn't yet reached the point of overt sado-masochism but it was obviously moving in that direction. Never in his wildest dreams – and he had written of many 'scenarios' a decade earlier – had he come to this point. What was more, this was no longer fiction. This was a living, breathing and beautiful reality. It was, to his mind, the next level of *Perfection*. If the word was overused then just so. What it meant though was every time it was used, it was raising the bar – the standard to a new level... of *Perfection*. Despite the early traumas, mixed with sublime sex, he really couldn't believe that such a physically gorgeous woman, with what appeared to be genuine emotion for him as well as a fantastic range of erotic ambitions, was willing to surrender herself to him. After all...

He made it clear, time and again, that he had no money (to squander); that every spare penny went to his family, to retain the home near New York and to maintain the girls at their chosen colleges in Scotland. (He suspected they preferred the US four-year undergraduate programme to what they considered the slighter English three-year model. In any case, they just wanted to be back in Britain for a while as well.)

Anyway, Lorraine had 'bowled-him-over'.

This is what your letter – your list – has done to me. (He sent her a picture of his erect manhood.)

The list is perfect – you *are* the creator but if more comes to mind, I shall share. The ultimate beauty, of course, is the opening... *'I want to be the source of your release, sexual and emotional release'.*

Oh my goodness! I am parched. I want that beautiful cock in my mouth! Truly horny now!

Masturbate with the dildo, dry, the extra friction. Close your eyes and pretend it's me pushing it in and out of you. Hear my voice in your head.

I might just do that but did you know that I have never used a dildo on myself? Did you get my pussy shot?

I don't think you realize how profoundly moving this list was and is to me. Beyond the simple physical acts of abuse, torture even (gagging for example because my cock is rammed straight down your throat so that you almost choke and vomit) and surrender to my latent sadism (why else would I enjoy such things and get an erection just writing this now to you?). It is the fact that you want me and only me to do all this to you and with you. No greater love has a woman for her man than to want to be subjected to this and suffer the pleasure of the pain that is associated with it. What am I to do, Lorraine, in that I feel as if you have been sent to me from the heavens? We have been tested, sorely tested, as we both know and have experienced, and yet you had the courage to keep trying and I found myself responding with increased belief and enthusiasm. Now to the point of your (not exhaustive) list of masochistic delights: with my initial reactions now *embedded* for each, you delicious walking cunt!

You may punish me. *Already stated; this is a sublime declaration of love!*

1. *I will give you my mouth and throat to use and abuse with your giant cock.* It shall be abused *(again) to the point of you choking. You shall lay upside down on your bed, with your head back, your mouth wide open and therefore your throat straight, its passage clear, allowing my cock to pass into its deepest recesses, past your immediate throat-point of resistance...*

2. *I will become your urinal when you get home. You shall sit or kneel, as the space allows. You shall open and keep your mouth open. I shall aim at your face and your mouth,*

ensuring that you consume each last drop, unless of course, you are released to pass some to my mouth, your dirty slut!

3. *I will consume copious amount of water so that I can give you streams and streams of piss whenever you demand it.* When demanded, I need your language to be bad, to be filthy, treating me with pissing contempt.

4. *My arse-hole will be cleaned and ready for your mouth.* My tongue yearns for the sensation of that opening. I need you to push even harder on to my tongue.

5. *I will lick your arse-hole clean and I will fuck you with a dildo to your satisfaction.* You are to do this slowly and with great purpose. You are to convey to me in words, your thoughts as you fuck me like a man would, you whore of whores.

6. *You can slap, spit, bite, pinch and choke me because I am a whore and whores need to be punished.* This is only the start of your punishments. At times it will be different such as when we are alone, I shall remain fully clothed while you are ordered to be and do everything completely naked and when the moment strikes, you shall be bent over a suitable item of furniture and taken, either from the front or behind, as the shape of the attack inspires me.

7. *I will not greedily swallow all the cum but remember to share it with you.* This is essential and conveys to you how much I adore you and want my cum to be returned to me from your sensual mouth.

8. *I shall not protest if you choose to fuck my pussy and a dildo in my ass at the same time.*

There is no possibility of protest. When the moment is right, it shall be done, with care initially and with force ultimately.

9. *I will gladly agree to be blind-folded, collared, spanked, whipped and abused for your contented pleasure.* Welts shall appear across your ass-cheeks, the backs of your legs and over your breasts.

10. *I will answer to piss, slut, whore, cunt, bitch names.* The names shall be repeated time and again, you fucking bitch!

I tried to compose a letter but it was not coming together beautifully and so I decided to send you a list (a bucket list). You can add more scenarios.

When more come to mind, I shall share them. When more come to your mind, you shall share also.

Your walking cunt! You are most certainly my walking cunt. You walk as if you know it and I shall remind you of it by whispering to you when you least expect it.

John continued:

Meanwhile, I need to stick a smooth, clean bottle into your cunt and keep it there, making you take over and speaking to me as you fuck yourself with it.

I shall tie you to your table, flat on your front, arms and legs wide apart (I've written this earlier) but in a torture sequence, you really shall be helpless and will be abused accordingly.

I shall tie you to the bed, flat on your back and find ways to drive you helpless with sex and fear. Pain shall be administered in doses that you can tolerate.

You utterly contemptible and complete woman. My woman; something I am still in disbelief about. -How can such a gorgeous woman select me as her mate, her man, her fuck partner in fucking and in life? I am so lucky. You are a treasure! Xxx

19.

I really don't know what to say to you except that I love you so much, that it is getting deeper and deeper and deeper. There is desperation and fear. 'Desperation' because I know I must wait but the wait is extremely hard to cope with. It must be done though because each day we express and learn a little more about each other. The 'fear' is as you fear: betrayal. As I mentioned earlier, I want to feel utterly and completely safe with you. What I am realizing (beyond your one hundred per cent agreement to my earlier assessment of some of your key phrases) is that we are the same; we mirror each other. You have an abject horror of betrayal. I have been betrayed; the most fundamental betrayal of all and have spent my life, since I was five, trying to come to terms with it. Just as I reached that point, in late 2014 (and definitely, better late than never), I have found you or better still, we have found each other. And as the other message (on torture items acknowledged), we have come through fire and hell to get to this point. If you believe in any kind of destiny, then just hope that our destiny is inextricably entwined and that nothing – and I mean *nothing* – is going to keep us apart. Simply put and often stated in other messages, 'I want to go to bed and fall asleep with you and I want to wake up with you and bring you tea, while I have coffee, as we talk gently and prepare for the day to come'. I wonder if you have any idea what you are doing to me. Do you? If I am doing the same to you, then we must take the greatest care of each other, in love and in our wilder ambitions.

For now then, Lorraine, remember what needs to be thought through:

1. A nice quiet restaurant for our first Saturday evening, where we can talk and talk some more?

2. A place where we can go the following weekend; away from Freetown?

3. Thinking (just thinking at this moment) about living arrangements; our options (we talk about this rather than writing about it. I want to see your expressions and the colour of your eyes as we do so).

I'm completely in love with you, Lorraine. I have let myself go. My heart is surrendered to you. Make it and me feel safe my love.

Love and more,

John xxx

P.S. I'm in New York City tomorrow morning. All the family will be in the house by the time I get back so not much tranquility for writing. I need to spend this rare time with them anyway. I yearn (as always) to read your thoughts, to see any pictures you might send (the lighting of your cunt was perfect so don't hesitate to try the other requested poses) and to open any hard core links (I'm saving the latest till all are asleep).

Bye, my pornographic priestess!

***

Then, as if completely unexpected...
Merry Christmas, baby!
I love you so much!
I am scared because I have never loved like this before.
I commit to you completely, my love.
I give you all of me and I will show you what real love is all about. Let me and I will show and give it to you. Come back to me.

My dearest love,

We have just spoken briefly. I'm so glad you've been with friends and you've had a lovely Christmas eve and early morning. I was so, so glad to hear from you too.

This love business is extremely powerful I understand the 'scared' bit; me too but I think it's a good scared, a caring scared so that neither of us wants to screw things up.

Let me share a Christmas picture. The open door is the room where I sleep. The wood-burning stove, to the right, is on. Presents have just been put under the tree. The bags you helped me choose are in that pile; thank you and thank you again!

I need you very much and I love you very much. It is all so exciting!

More tomorrow, my angel (and I sent you a second card earlier, which you appear not to have opened) xxx

I am your man and I want to feel the totality of that real love. Soon we shall be living it, in all its wonderful and extreme aspects. Never let that spirit within you die!

Thank you for sharing your home photos with me. Your home looks warm and loving. I miss wood burning; it goes with the Christmas spirit.

I need you too, the whole you, I don't know how we are going to do it but I need you in my bed every night. I need you to need me; I will love and protect you in return.

Merry Xmas, my sweetest love!

20.

SLAVE; addendum to our DECLARATION: Lorraine hereby agrees and confirms, without equivocation, hesitation and with her own free will, to enter into this pact of slavery, as follows:

1.   She will do as she is ordered to do at all times, in all matters of sex.

2.   She shall open each orifice as is required by her man (John) whether she is enthusiastic at that moment or not.

3.   She shall never, repeat never say no, ever.

4.   She shall suck his cock even if he has not requested it.

5.   She shall push one, two or even three fingers in his ass, even if he has not requested it.

6.   She shall lie, sit, stand, bend over or in any other contortion, accept his sexual desire.

7.   She shall be raped, at the appropriate time.

8.   She shall be whipped, at the appropriate time.

9.   She shall be spat upon at the appropriate time.

10. She shall be pissed upon at the appropriate time.

11. She shall be really and truly fucked whether she hungers for it or not.

12. She shall comply with all other twisted requirements (one of which has to be revealed later today).

Please confirm your acceptance, freely, willingly and enthusiastically, to this addendum to our Declaration.

I, Lorraine, hereby freely and willingly (enthusiastically) confirm and agree on all the written orders. I will obey you with no hesitation.

PS: what about when I need to rest, read, talk to you?

Baby! The slavery is only at the appropriate times! When I am in heat, whether you are or not (part of the essence of the slave agreement). More later, my gorgeous woman!

My love!

Thanks for the warm reply. I'll get back to you on some matters raised, later. I will also check the hotel and get back to you on that too.

Question:

In the absence of a bidet, after I've had a shit, I run the warm water tap (cold if there is no warm water) and use my finger to wash the actual shit hole. After the rim is clean, I push the same finger in to ensure that everything is clean. I withdraw a few times. Brown colour becomes paler and paler until there is nothing. All is absolutely clean. I then push in one more time for a sensual, fucking sensation. Then the little ritual is finished. Question: rather than my finger; would you be willing to perform this act of sensual kindness and gesture to total intimacy and care?

Oh, my honey, I will lovingly (occasionally) do it for you while sensually kissing you. Of course!

We both understand that we are pushing the boundaries beyond the norm. If we were looking from the outside (as strangers), it would be judged (possibly) as contemptible but we love it.

She took pictures of her cunt.

I can't do better than this; it's awkward taking with an iPad. I keep blocking the camera!

They were delicious.

Do you have any idea at all what this does for me about you? Do you? It shows me that you are my total woman. That you are willing to do anything for me – your man – because you are my woman. It is a gesture to total trust and surrender to which you open yourself up, literally, allowing your cunt to be photographed and sent to me: such an intimate confirmation of sex and love. The funny thing is that when you see all the pictures you have sent to me, the sub-folder 'self' starts with two pictures of my cock, followed immediately by these three of your cunt. I didn't do the order. It's just how the numbering arranged itself. Then I looked again, closely, and imagined that I was already burying my face in there and thrusting my tongue into this most secret and sacred place. It is sacred and deserves to be treated as such. It is sacred because you have bequeathed it, in its entirety, to me. It is also sacred because it is the fount of all ultimate pleasure; it is what drives a man crazy for (the various methods of) penetration and drives a woman crazy in her hunger for her man's cock, his tongue and his fingers. Thank you for doing this, my angel of desire, beautifully wicked, and frankly, again just *Perfection!*

My Sweetest Love!

This is the best mail yet I have received from you! The way you convey your feelings in words is so so beautiful! Which girl would not get wet to such? You impress me with so much about you, how can I not want. You and your all, would anyone blame me? I don't think so. You complete me in so many ways yet I know that we have work to do if this is ever going to flourish. I have faith that it can and it will. I hope you agree.

(John sent her a black-and-white picture of a woman tied spread-eagled to a dining table, with the cutlery and crockery still in place. She was blindfolded. The man was not in full view but he was dressed, the shirt sleeves terminating in folded cuffs and cuff-links. Champagne flutes stood to attention as the picture captured the sight of the obviously hot wax on her sumptuous breasts and nipples.)

At home, alone. Will take a shower then think deeply of how to respond to the torture, sweet pain (candle) that unexpectedly made me wet.

I want to be ravaged so much (by you).

21.

If you looked at it in a twisted way, wouldn't you agree that, our almost losing each other has been the greatest thing that could have happened? Ponder on that, my love.

No need to ponder. Your insight is perfect as your body, you cunt and your mind is the dirtiest and most deliciously pornographic mind I have ever encountered! For example, while I have occasionally wondered about candles, I have never, repeat never, had the opportunity to share the thought, the scenario or the agreement.

My pornographic lover and partner: there is so much that has passed between us in writing these past two weeks. I shall print each 'conversation' so that I can read, re-read and highlight those key passages that are helping to build the word picture of my Lorraine's inner being. The reading will start when I am sitting in JFK in two weeks' time (two weeks today), and continue while I wait at Brussels airport for the other plane, back to Freetown and you.

As promised earlier, the punishment-torture item I forgot shall come later. I need solitude with time, to compose properly. You may not like it but that'll be too bad. In slave mode, you will have no alternative.

Meanwhile, more cunt pictures would be more than just welcomed. They would be drooled over.

Thank you for this letter. I am just gulping and slightly trembling waiting to read about my torture item. Mmmh... trembling in anticipation. Cunt pictures to be taken and sent to you later. On another note, I have been checking some places for our getaway, when you get back.

We go there and, with our month of writing reconstruction, we shall start again, without weed and without excessive drinking and without any pre-planning of erotic sequences. What shall unfold shall simply unfold, including the peeling back of your pussy lips (the unfolding) to allow my tongue deeper entry into you most secret space!

I would like the getaway weekend to symbolize our rebirth and a start of a great partnership. There will be no excessive anything apart from our excessive lust for each other. We shall just let everything flow. I hunger for you.

My baby! This is perfect; thanks so much! Remember to reinforce resident rates for me too! Meanwhile, imagine this.

You are lying there. The picture does not convey it but your hands and feet are tied; you cannot move. You are afraid but you thrill at the prospect of punishment; torture, even. You are wicked. You have been a bad woman and your behaviour needs to be corrected; it must be. Then there is the slave agreement. Punishment is the first part but this is torture. You are a slave and as such, you are the object of your master's pleasure and this is my pleasure at this particular moment.

All is quiet. The flat is empty. Screaming is therefore permitted and expected. You beg for release. The begging is ignored. You are kissed on your lips. You cannot resist. You are kissed on your cunt. You cannot resist. You use a soft voice as if to seduce me into mercy. It does not work. The candle is revealed. It is red; the devil's colour. Matches are presented. The box is shaken by your ear. You flinch in fear. The box is opened, a match is taken out and struck. The candle is lit. It takes time to form some liquid wax. While waiting, your ear is licked. You can't stand that mixture of sex and tickling. The wax is ready. The candle is taken, it is tilted forward and the first drops fall, first on your right breast, then your left...

I say yes to the candle torture. I could only take it from you! You make it sound so devilishly delicious! Oh please be all dressed up when I am tied up and all exposed; my head is ecstatic intellectually, my body thrilled emotionally, at the prospect.

My god, Lorraine! You've added yet another dimension; that I am dressed up. For you (and only for you), I may even put on a tie!

Dark glasses might be included as well. My pleasure and surprise in all this is that you have actually agreed to the candle treatment with relish, you twisted cunt. And, of course, I am your twisted man!

You in a tie and dark glasses. What a delightful image. I see me all trussed up, scared and very wet, wondering what the beautiful beast will do to me next...
I love your mind.

There is, of course, in some scene or other, you blindfolded...

Oh baby, I will trust you, I do trust you.
What you do to me with words alone is a thrill in itself; knowing that I have tasted your heavy balls, your erect massive pulsating, hard as steel cock, your very tasty pre-cum that I still hunger for more, your squeaky-clean tasty and velvety arse-hole, your flat abs, your nipples, your face and your delectable hungry mouth. As I was saying, knowing I have experienced all that and I am to get that and much more (now that we have opened up to each other), is making me very impatient.

Two weeks today, at your time, I shall be in your arms, whether in your taxi, your shower, your table or your bed. Just remember again, that I will have moved and travelled for twenty-four hours: I may be bursting with hunger or exhaustion. Either way, you'll know how to take care of me!

Now that we have opened up to each other, my angel, you have an emotional intelligence well beyond your years. And yes, we have opened up to each other on equal terms and with equal trust, expressing anything and everything that we desire for ourselves in pleasure and porn. -Love simply blossoms in this context!

Shirt:

I have a shirt. It is so worn that I saw for the first time, after it had been washed, that it is now torn at one shoulder. This is good. One day, or evening, you shall wear it but with nothing else on. It shall drop, roughly to your pussy-line. Depending on how the event proceeds, you may be tickled, teased or even slightly abused – in slave mode. But there will come a point when I shall be seized with rage and passion, wanting to tear into you and rip you open, let alone apart. At that point, the shirt shall be ripped from you, torn apart, the tearing being a metaphor – reflecting my tearing hunger for you!

Oh Jesus, John!

Do not doubt it. This will happen at the appropriate time... It might even be vicious...

Reading from you always has me sopping wet. Jesus, John! How will we survive the trip from the airport to my house?

It's an interesting thought! Are we using Fred? (Their regular cab driver.)

No. I will get a better cab that night, comfortable and with no familiar ears listening to our sexy conversations.

Get a woman driver. Then I will comfortably fall to my knees to taste your cunt, or for you to do the same to me.

I actually have a good woman cab driver with a very nice car but no falling on your knees or we might find ourselves on the roadside!

In that case, wear a skirt or dress with no panties, so that I can at least caress your pussy with my fingers, licking them from time to time...

The thought makes me hunger for you more and more, achingly so. You have a devilish mind; truly delicious!

Don't hesitate to identify clothes of yours that are no longer needed. Confirm that the item is no longer required and that you are at my mercy. I shall then know whether to attack immediately or sometime later but in either case, at a moment that you simply won't anticipate (unless you see my eyes turn to one of pure lust).

I will show you clothes that can be ripped.
When I wear them, you can decide at your own
time, when to attack (I so want you to attack me;
without mercy, viciously. John, I need this from
you!) Can you imagine what I would be going
through? Jumpy, scared and horny at the same
time, not knowing when you would attack.

Precisely so, my love, as I stare at your three pussy pictures again. Thank you, my collection of your photos is growing, so much more for me to drool over.

He sent her his latest mug-shot. He'd had a haircut.

Oh my! You have not shaved. You look
absolutely hot!

For you, I shall be unshaven after a week on Monday morning, so an entire working week of growth, just for your flesh-tearing pleasure!

Even I was quite flattered when I saw the pictures; shows what a decent haircut can do with a head shape like mine.

If it is possible to love you even more, then consider it so. In any case, I'm going to try and capture that idea in words for you later today (to greet you tomorrow morning). Certain ideas are forming which must be captured in this unfolding narrative...

Let me check your other messages, know that you are on my mind constantly and that I shall be composing for you later tonight (my time). Meanwhile, the three current 'recent photos' are two of your pussy and the spanking marks on that ass (the picture which you copied). Have you masturbated yet with the dildo?

Love and more, my pornographic bitch!

Thank you for the nice words, as always and my bottom cannot wait to feel the sharp sting of your hands. We will break through, no worries about that. The question is, how long can my cunt stay without your cock; torturous moments indeed!

In that case, my love, take a picture of the dildo inserted in your cunt, then use it as often as is necessary, until I return to you. Read the message (earlier) that ends with the request for you not to wear panties when you meet me.

If I find a fitting dress to be seen with at the airport, I will not wear anything underneath.
It will take time before I get wet for a dildo, do you understand? Does it make sense?

My baby! The fitting dress with nothing underneath sounds (and will look) perfect. Even as I read and reply, my cock responds. If you feel unable to 'get wet', use the baby oil to lubricate that most beautifully secret place.

Love and porn in abundance,

John

22.

This is what I responded to you eight hours ago. 'Agreed, you fucking bitch! So much agreed.' Your phrase *'we are more emotionally connected'* highlights not only your own 'emotional maturity, well beyond you years' but also, harbours the portent of what I am going to write to you later tonight. Good girl!

It's that highlighted phase that is important. For me, it represents the second level of our foundation. The first (whether you like it or not) is pure sex: clean, dirty, exploitive, sadomasochistic and all manner of pleasures therein. It feels so comfortable; so correct, knowing that I have found my soulmate in this matter. This makes me feel deeply happy. I can't express in words what absolute joy it is to know that your mind and mine and therefore your body and mine, want – and indeed crave – the same thing in that fundamental pleasure of terrific sex, especially when we know that too many in this world deny that basic truth. This is my first reason for wanting to be with you. It is how we started and the possibilities are what have carried us through the early difficulties (a gentle phrase that hides so much early pain).

The second level then is the 'emotional connection'. These past two weeks have been crucial in this regard. We have worked our way through a series of thoughts which have brought us to a level of trust that simply has to be confirmed in reality. That works for us both. It is not going to be denied and you have already acknowledged it – the need to work it through. We know that we both still have vulnerabilities – on the emotional level – but we also know that we both want this to work, in the context of love; an unshakeable love - an unbreakable love. We shall prove this to ourselves and to each other... and, indeed, to the world!

It's the third level that raises interesting points in my mind. As I've written: the porn stuff is solid (and in need of endless experience). The love part is strong and growing daily (as we exchange more thoughts with each other). It's the intellectual side of things that has recently occurred to me. The very idea of you and me has entered my thoughts. Stepping back a little and looking in wonder... or amazement, even. It is that feeling – elation perhaps – that teases my mind. Is this real? Can it work? This gorgeous woman who wants me! Intellectually, I know it can work. I also know that if the gods are with us, it will work. As an idea, therefore, this third level of understanding is very important. It gives a rationale or credence to the first and second levels above. It's real, it's workable and it's very, very exciting!

Finally then: a promise, if it is in my gift to offer it. I have no intention to be willingly apart from you for four weeks again. No, no, NO! This time has been (and is) important as we heal ourselves and develop confidence at all three levels. For example, I suspect that for my birthday, I shall be with my girls in England then pop over to NY to see my boys. That will take a week or so. It's my second week (that I usually take) that I would like to do something really nice with you, to go somewhere for up to a week...

I love you so, so much. Outsiders would say that I am mad and that I love you too, too much. They are fools and do not understand the spirit that flies between us on all three levels It is still growing and will continue for as long as we are alive together.

I still can't believe that we have met, what we've been through, where we are now and the thrilling possibilities that lie ahead. Thank you, Lorraine, for being you and for wanting me so much.

Your man in love and all other delights – polite and less so!

She replied:

I feel completely the same way, my love, and yes, our initial attraction to each other was just pure lust. I was attracted at first to your dirty mind and when I met you, your fucking sexy demeanour and later, mind blowing sex and more of that! So, yes, it's been about sex until we almost lost each other, and through our pornographic and emotional emails, we have been able to connect emotionally, and to tell you the truth, this is the first time I have felt so, and it feels good to know you. I feel genuinely protective of you. I am in love with you which at first, wasn't even on my mind. As the ad you responded to stated: I wanted a man '...who is not looking for a LTR but for a lady friend to enjoy fantasy trials with'.

We will be fine, John, if we want it to work, it will. Yes we have some work to do, I would like our time together to be full of laughter, pornographic sex, love and care, no more, no less.

Could you please explain to me the third phase, please? I don't think I quite understood...

I am excited about the trips that are popping up everywhere; a week would be heaven, away from people and only with you. Talking about you is making me a little anxious, what with two more weeks to go. After seeing that handsome face after the haircut, I can't get your sexy face out of my mind!

Come home, I want to love you like I have never loved before. Will you be able to handle it?

Explain the third phase? Simple. Step outside yourself and just think; not feel, not masturbate, just think about the idea of us. It is beyond sex and beyond emotion. It is simply the *idea* of us. It is a very good idea. I'm thinking about the idea of us a lot; clearer? If not, I'll try again.

'I want to love you like I have never loved before. Will you be able to handle it?' Certainly, if all that we have written about comes true; comes to fruition. The real question is 'will Lorraine be able to handle it?'

As for our recent analyses: I think we have reached a point where we must now just settle into each other and live the reality, armed with the ideas shared; emotional and pornographic; nothing speaks louder than the actual doing, the actual living.

Finally, my pornographic priestess: I have not looked at porn sites for at least a decade or so. There was a time (around 1999-2001) when I was addicted. The point about then was that the sites themselves were very poor compared to the quality of pictures and streaming that you have introduced to me. I am therefore going to dip in a little deeper – and when I find something that I think is genuinely hot, I shall share it with you – and I want you to continue sharing hot stuff with me. But and this is an important 'but': you must understand that when I was porn addicted then, I hOad no one to share with. I was using the images I found to inspire some writing. That's the crucial difference between then and now. Now, I have you to share all this stuff with; frankly, a pure and wonderful concept.

Take me, protect me and keep me.

Yes, I have thought of us, deeply and further and I love us. We are good together, at least I feel that way. There's so much more to learn about each other. If you ask me, I would rather I get on with knowing everything about you and you me, so we can get back on with our pornographic, erotic lives. Wouldn't you agree, my honey?

We will find ways of making this work, getting closer, never getting dissuaded, being patient with each other, loving each other. Everything else would then just flow.

I hope I am not enabling you with your former porn addiction. (I certainly hope not. If yes, then I say; John! Stop watching porn!)

I sure hope I can share anything with you and you with me; I hope so.

I am your walking cunt priestess!

He responded, slightly, just slightly concerned.

I hope I am not enabling you with your former porn addiction. (I certainly hope not. If yes, then I say; John! Stop watching porn!) Silly girl! This is rekindling thoughts for you and me - nothing to do with secrets and exclusions. I won't do it unless each picture and video was for you and me, you and me, you and me! Do you understand that?

I sure hope I can share anything with you and you with me; I hope so. I fucking hope so too, Lorraine. You are my dream woman at last, at last, at fucking last!

I am your walking cunt priestess! That you most certainly are, whether walking, flat on your back with legs wide apart or restrained. You cannot move and I am doing interesting things to you and with you...

23.

Just checked the card. Although I type into the full screen, when sent, it is expanded. This time, I take the precaution of copying the entire message.

In contrast to the two earlier pictures of an (implied) sophisticated gentleman, punishing his slave with the subtlety of exquisite torture, this is the other extreme: dirty, degrading and lots of wax over the front of your body. You delight and even thrill in entertaining these wide-ranging possibilities and (for heaven's sake!) I seem to relish the thought of administering the punishment (I wonder why?). You are for me the perfect woman, in ideas, in love and in all manner of sexual deviation. Again and again, thank you for being you and thank you for wanting and hungering after me!

'I seem to relish the thought of administering punishment (I wonder why?)', you ask. You tell me. I seem to enjoy the prospects and the little we have tried.

I love the way you call me 'slut, cunt, whore, bitch, my walking cunt and the best, my woman!'

I seem to enjoy the almost savage affection we have for each other and the animalistic instincts we bring in and out of each other. I love this new me and, believe me, it's very new! I have been aware of how I feel. How I have exposed myself to situations (relationships) where I knew that it would be an option, did it (but it's not the same). I was always angry about one thing or another but wanted to please and with my always 'sadistic' mind hovering, wanted to test too and see if I would like it (it's another beautiful girl, for the gods' sake!). I can promise you, I never really got into it, wanted to very much but never did, and it's because of the disconnection. There was no partnership, no trust and I never missed to ask myself what I was doing there. (You should be here next to me so I could narrate it to you.) In my previous relationship, we even had a proper threesome and the last one turned into my nightmare. I could have died from heartache and yet I know, in every inch of me, that it's going to be our making and it's going to be beautiful. Typing that has made me wet.

As you said: 'this feels correct'. I concur: it feels like I have never felt before. I feel like I belong to you. I feel loved gently and roughly with love. You even love (tolerate) my edges. You love me the same: you brought me tea to bed even after a fight and with so much kindness in your eyes (I am tearing up remembering that). You *make me feel like a woman. I feel so proud when walking with you, my handsome man.*

I will love and protect you. You don't need me, you have me!

Wow! Let me get back to this in about an hour... it merges with other thoughts I wanted to share about what's going on with me. My bit will come first then embedding.

This is what I wanted to respond to hours earlier but never had the solitude. Now I have. Let me embed first then offer more text but before that...

I looked again at your most recent picture; stunning, really sexy, beautiful, and again I still can't believe that a woman with your looks and hidden desires, settles on me but I welcome it. I appreciate it. Frankly, I love it!

Now, reactions to your text:

I seem to enjoy our almost savage affection we have for each other and the animalistic instincts we bring in and out of each other. *First, it is something I relish; the freedom and trust to be able to share such ideas with each other, knowing that every thought is one that is not merely a thought but a prelude to action, stuff in real life; sweaty, thrusting, at times gentle and at others, really savage. A good word for you to introduce; a good word for us to use!*

I love this new me and believe me, it's very new! *It's this that I find so hard to believe at first - the word 'new'. Me thinking that your previous relationships have been at the level of ours, with freedom of thought, expression and action – then I read... and with my always 'sadistic' mind, wanted to test and see if I would like it* (it's another beautiful girl, for the gods' sake!) I never really got into it, wanted to very much... *I begin to understand you more and more and more because of what you are conveying here. Do you understand that I am understanding you more and more? You wanted to very much but it wasn't right. It was a wrong connection. Now, with me, you know there is a solid connection and therefore now, not only can you want to very much but also, you can do so with confidence because our minds are the same on this. Your expression and desire for pushing the boundaries are my expression and desire as well. Wonderful!*

...we have even had a proper threesome and the last one turned into my nightmare... and yet I know, with every inch of me, that it's going to be our make and it's going to be beautiful; typing that has me wet. *My dearest love. Next time we shall love it and love each other.... yes, at your call, at your command!*

I feel like I belong to you... *As far as I'm concerned, you do belong to me; you are mine, I possess you (as you do me). You are my woman and that makes me feel terrific.*

I will love and protect you. You don't need me, you have me! *This sentence carries so much. My heart leaps because of it! Xxx*
Later, love.

And now for my additional text, in normal script!

I've suggested this before in previous messages and I am going to say it again. I want you to be clear in what I tell you. Yes, I thought you had a series of relationships and in each one, you were at the level of understanding, love and the sharing of pornography that we have reached. You keep telling me of your eventual disappointments. I don't care with whom, what and where all this happened and frankly, I do not want to know. What I do want to know and I think I now understand is that there are two aspects or two words or phrases that emerge from your experiences to date. First, you have been *betrayed*. Secondly, you have never felt totally *free to express* the ideas you have, the sado-masochistic stuff... Even more fundamentally perhaps, you have *never received* the same free-flowing ideas from your previous partners as you have received (and welcomed with great enthusiasm) from me. Let's look again at each key word or phrase.

BETRAYED: whatever happened, you were betrayed. You put your trust in the partner(s) you were with and they cheated. Again, I do not want to know the details. All I want to know is that if I believe in you, there is no way on earth I would ever threaten or betray that belief. I would and will not do anything to fuck up our rapidly growing relationship, partnership and fundamental love bond. What we must simply do now is let the experience of living catch up with (what will turn out to be) a month of writing with powerful revelations: emotional and deeply pornographic, both of which we want to devour with passion and, at times, ferocity.

FREEDOM TO EXPRESS: this is a fundamental requirement for me and for you. I need and want you to express every fucking idea you can think of. I did so earlier (fucking you through your period). You said 'no'; perfectly understandable and I have absolutely no problem with that. You must say 'no' if that is what you feel. The point is, you have developed in me a basic belief in you; that I can express anything with you, about you and to you. I love to do so. You have now opened up to me more and more, using pictures to very, very good effect! You started with your history (earlier pictures), then illustrated with some of your dream images – S&M

included – then moved on to erotic poses of yourself, including of your delicious cunt. I keep on saying 'delicious' because that's what it is: in touch, oral texture and taste. Again, I thought this was not new for you but you tell me that you have never been able to express such thoughts so freely, with any partner. Then, this is one more area that you, me and we will blossom.

YOUR PARTNER'S IDEAS: a little repetition perhaps but worth acknowledging. If the traffic was mostly one way before (you to him), it is now two-way. In my case, previously, I had to channel my writing into books. Now, I have the absolute joy of sharing and expressing with you, ideas in words and (at present) Kinky Cards, and images of a sophisticated gentleman (with tie) torturing quietly with hot candle-wax, his woman, his slut, his slave, his whore, his complete and perfect walking cunt. This is what you are to me (as I express and repeat) your partner's (John's) ideas to you. This is *Perfection*. There is no other word for it.

My Savage!

You got me right! I have never been able to express, I almost gave up on this lifestyle because of so much selfishness. That's why they say that you should be sure and stable emotionally, understanding boundaries and rules and respecting them. Yes, it's been a journey: a tortuous month indeed but I am grateful because through the thorns we have been able to emerge to our true carnal senses. I am truly grateful for all the mails and erotic photos and videos that we have a shared. It's been thrilling but I want my savage back. Yes, you are my sophisticated gentleman who tortures me too and I absolutely love it!

Torture me, my male whore! I am so excited.

Please let's make it work! It's good for both of us!

My perfect John!

Hold on...

She decided to express freely; testing her new freedom?

Will you let me watch porn when I want to?

Will you put your cock into me even when asleep?

Will you sit on my face and threaten to go potty on my face?

Will you spit in my mouth?

Will you stick a dildo in my pussy while you fuck my ass?

Will you let me love you?

Will you shove your cock deep down my throat and choke me at the same time?

Will you shove your cock deep in my ass?

Will you please rape me unannounced? Roughly and savagely? Please?

Will you promise to hold me tight after all such ordeals?

24.

The New Year heralded a new start...

Happy New Year, my dearest love!

It's just turned midnight here. Now I go to bed. I'll wake between six and seven a.m., between one and two p.m. your time. I'll call as soon as I wake up.

We have so much to look forward to in 2015.

Much love and so much delicious wickedness!

Your man, John.

My love, my love! I am looking forward to our New Us: the New Year with someone that I truly love and adore, and to our mutual love of wicked ideas! How I am looking forward to our time together, exploration and so much more. You occupy most of my thoughts. I hunger for you, desperately!

My baby, I know how you feel because I feel exactly the same. The time of analyzing endlessly as we sometimes have done (which was absolutely necessary) is drawing to a close. We have reached a level of understanding that now must be turned into a living, loving and fucking reality, with all our joyful and filthy ideas thrown in! It's going to be good!

She sent seven erotic poses of herself; a sort of New Year gift...

My god! I just can't believe, yet again, how stunning you are! Then you even stuff the dildo into your asshole, getting it ready for the real thing to come. I now have an exquisite collection of pictures of you; obviously, some are quite hard to take! You can indeed ease off now and instead, when you feel inclined, share pictures of scenes you would like to see replicated with or by you, such as the first black-and-white ones (example here). Love to my beautiful sex creature! Are you really human?

Seven more pictures came; of various golden showers.

Then, as I reply to the pictures of you, and suggest you send some other images of what you like, you do so (because I am opening your emails in the order I received them). I'm going to piss on you when the bladder and cock co-operate and you are definitely going to do the same to me!

I love you dearly, Lorraine. I love you passionately, Lorraine. I love you pornographically, my delicious walking whore cunt!

I want all of that too, John. As you stated earlier, 'we just have to live it now', to test our emotional theories.
I will faithfully wait for your phone call. It will mean so much to me. I want to take care of you, I will take care of you, I will love you... we have to live it. I am going back to my masturbation, if I can. I will wait for my card.
I love you with all my being!

I hope by now that you are asleep. When we come together more and more often during the forthcoming weeks, I must have a reasonable amount of sleep! By Easter (if not sooner), other living decisions will be taken.

Just remember: I want to find myself in the position, with confidence, that I can go to bed with you, fuck you in various ways (if that is our mutually consenting pleasure, and sometimes when I have to take you against your initial will), then fall asleep, stay asleep then wake up to your intoxicating body and filthy mind. However, if I wake up in the dead of night and feel like it, I shall lick my fingers, massage your cunt till I sense you can welcome me, then I shall slide my cock into you so that you think you are in a dirty dream but no, it's your dirty John, just fucking you for the exquisite pleasure that you give him, time and again, in words, sentiments, pictures and reality.

I am yours.

You should definitely have enough sleep now that you will be back to work. I don't know how that is going to happen with our new discovered love and lust for each other!

I cannot promise you calm or complete peace when you come over for a sleepover since I don't live here alone and this house has people streaming throughout. We will just have to see how things pan and enjoy the moments we get together, I can take that, if I have you fully. I am fine with the arrangements. What about you?

I want you to take me even when asleep, you dirty beast! I miss that!

Thank you for the card. Maybe the red candle day should be when we are away for a first weekend in our New Year spirit?

Relax, Lorraine! Things will be sorted. Weekends, I don't care about sleep. I care more about quality fucking with my slut cunt woman! Weekdays are another matter but we'll work it out!

I miss you so much, whether dreaming about wax all over your breasts or not. We shall select a range of possibilities to take with us when going to Mombasa for that initial weekend. The possibilities, not pre-planning, mad woman!

Take a deep breath, relax again and confess to me if you did or did not release your horniness with good 'self-abuse' (masturbation). Delicious, my angel! Truly delicious!

I am not worried about the arrangements; we will be fine.

I am truly looking forward to you coming back and that first weekend out, I am not planning but I can't help but wonder in excitement, what we will be up to.

I have not made plans for post-New Year. I never do but Alice is suggesting going away. I have a feeling we will not but I am keeping quiet lest new plans come up. I would really rather stay at home. I will let you know but will definitely wait for that sexy voice.

Mmmh, I did come to your cock image! Hard! -With your growling voice behind my ear. (It's my new cumming scenario; my little secret.) I am terribly sore from days of masturbating. I should take a rest but I get horny every now and then; more than before and it's your fault! Delicious fault!

This really is delicious but if your cunt is sore when I get back, you really will be punished! The fucking will be intense for us and painful for you!

I understand about no real plans for New Year. I will write a separate message in about an hour or so.

Pain or no pain, I want that cock impaling me!

I now have twenty-two pictures in the sub-folder 'self' - four of your delicious cunt, four of my cock and fourteen with various poses, where I can see your face along with so much more. Your sex and desire is pouring from each one. Heaven knows how we'll cope in the first forty-eight hours... What a delightful thought! For your information: the other two folders are 'dreams'; your deeply erotic thoughts, through pictures of others and 'history', all pictures shared before you started on the explicit range. How on earth can you be so hot? The latest positively sizzles! I am so lucky to know you, to have slept with you and to be able to continue sleeping with you in future.

I cherish every praise you give me. That you find me hot is a turn on by itself! I am proud to have slept with you since the first time we saw each other.

That's a lovely sentiment. It shall be cherished as an idea and put into practice, in reality! Love to the beautiful, gorgeous Lorraine.

Thank you, my Man!

25.

I do not want to fear you cheating on me, I am going to leave it at that and we will just have to prove to each other, that there's no other way.

John didn't understand this outburst 'out of the blue'. The other Lorraine had appeared again. Alarm bells should have started ringing. It was – it seemed – a permanent undercurrent. Nobody likes to be 'cheated' or to learn about a cheater. Yet, in the delicious Lorraine's case, it was more about a fundamental betrayal.

John knew about his own sense of fundamental betrayal; it had contorted his entire life. He started wondering if there was a similar incident in Lorraine's early life or that it was just a series of men. In any case, he didn't want to know about all that. Instead, he reasoned that if only he could prove, in fact – in living reality – that there was no intention 'to cheat' because he now possessed – at her insistence – the entirety of women in her. She was everything he could have – and indeed, had for many years – wished for. She was *all* women to him.

There were certainly some rough edges: smoking, drinking copiously at times and weed. He had never smoked, drank modestly – when living alone, perhaps an average of one beer or glass of wine a week (even his army discharge papers remarked on his 'sobriety') – and as for weed, he tried once when he was still playing club rugby. He was violently sick, slept, woke, wondering if he would ever be strong enough to play again, got on to his motorbike, went home (the weed was at a student friend's flat), showered, had coffee and a plate of baked beans, went to the toilet, farted like a broken jet engine, had more coffee, realized he was well again, jumped back on to his bike and sped to Ruislip, where he was due to play that afternoon. He played like a man-machine and was lauded for his performance at the end of the match; certainly ironic.

Will you let me watch porn when I want to? What a question to ask me! Of course BUT must it be exclusive to you.

My sweetheart!
I would like it very much if we could watch porn together but I am aware of your 'addiction' and would not want to be an enabler to you backsliding. Can you handle it?

You have touched a raw nerve. I was using the word 'addiction' in a playful way. If I was addicted I would have been overpowered by it years ago and continued to be so. I simply enjoy it immensely because we are sharing in the pleasure. I'm afraid to say that if I find you excluding me from anything (apart from things like going away to buy a present – innocent stuff), it will kill us! I absolutely hate the idea of exclusion!

This is what happened to me in my previous relationship, going to parties without me because she... "needed some breathing space." My glorious addiction is to you, not to porn. When I accused you of treating me like an 'appendage', that was a hint of feeling like I was being excluded, just being entertained at your whim.

If I sense that exclusion is to be an option at times (except for things like work), I shall close off, for my own protection! Do you understand this?

Do you want me to exclude you from such intimate, personal stuff; stuff that we both get immense enjoyment from?

I feel myself getting deeply upset because of this possibility; you excluding me when you choose to watch porn without me (when I'm in your presence, when I'm actually with you).

Sorry, Lorraine, but this is deadly serious. You've touched upon something that I cannot deal with, cannot cope with – exclusion.

I'm just up; my mind is razor sharp.

Please correct or address my deep-seated fear!

I will reply to your mails in a bit. I am just from the market with Alice's sister and I have a terrible allergy (dry throat and congested head). It usually disappears in a few hours, so I will go take a shower, tea and come and write to my sensitive honey.

PS: Exclusion has never been my intention... calm down.

Good brief reply, sweetie!

He called her.

Lovely to talk to you. Candles have been bought!

Candles will be painfully, erotically enjoyed!
I hope they are red!

I am gasping at the strings that held your voice over the phone. How beautiful! How so wonderfully gruff!

The candles are white, a perverted innocence. Let me get one or two red ones. More later my woman to be tortured, with grace and control... and to watch your body writhe and to hear your screams of passion and pain!

Will you let me watch porn when I want to?
What a question to ask me! Of course, but must it be exclusive to you.

Well of course it 'must be exclusive to me' and you, you and me, and us together in our agreed delicious lifestyle. You're fantastic. John, you are responsible for bringing out the embedded stored away, naughty Lorraine and for that, my love, I am grateful.

And I am so grateful to have met you and gone through everything we have so far to the point that I have liberated 'naughty Lorraine'. Is that not a fantastic feeling for you and a really rewarding feeling for me? You now have freedom to express and explore. Boundaries are acknowledged. In fact, I am going to update our mutual declaration with the additions / or amendments, if you want to use the U.S. declaration of independence analogy. I'll try doing that on Sunday (as well as seeing if there are red candles available...).

Honey! How was I to know that you were in jocular mood when telling me that you had an addiction? Seriously? I believed you and I realised my mistake when you replied. Why would I exclude you from watching porn with me, from talking about my cravings and fantasies with you, sharing everything with one rare human being that I deeply care about? John, wouldn't that defeat the purpose of being in this lifestyle in the first place? Isn't being free and open (with boundaries, of course) and not having inhibitions, be they physical or emotional, oh, and letting all our animalistic instincts let loose? I understand all this. Why would I want to exclude you? Please tell me?

It would not make sense for my head to ever think of excluding you from my devious ideas in my mind. Why would I want to be with you if I couldn't do that? Please understand that.

When you first mentioned 'I felt like an appendage', that hurt some.

I have not done that to you since we met and I have not excluded you from anyone, any event, nothing! I am sorry what you went through; I have my scars too. I can only offer you my devotion and love and hopefully it will erase most if not all the scars. I want to do that for you!

You are a lovely and deeply loving woman! Thank you so much for taking the time to explain all this and more – more understanding, more mutual care. I just needed that raw nerve – exposed – to be understood by you. And by the way, I know at least one of your raw nerves and the awful consequences of it before we had time to build up the other side of our mutual understanding. You are gorgeous and I love you as well as the idea of you... and as already mentioned elsewhere, candles (two fat ones, to allow the wax to gather as advised on a site I read), before letting the still hot wax drop on your skin and seeing it jump a little and hearing your muffled scream and groans of pain and pleasure combined, you beast woman!

26.

John then settled down and returned to some of her other delicious questions that needed replies...

Will you put your cock into me even when asleep? Yes!

Will you sit on my face and threaten to go potty on my face? What happens if potty comes accidentally? In truth, this did not kindle a spark of pleasure on his side.

Will you spit in my mouth? I shall hold your nose so that your mouth must open to accept my spit – lots of it!

Will you stick a dildo in my pussy while you fuck my ass? Certainly!

Will you let me love you? I need that more than anything!

Will you shove your cock deep down my throat and choke me at the same time? There is no question, this shall be done!

Will you shove your cock deep in my ass? This is an essential item!

Will you please rape me unannounced? Roughly and savagely? Please? You fucking animal!

When the moment is right, it shall be done and you shall have no inkling as to when. The more you resist, the harsher it shall be!

Will you promise to hold me tight after these ordeals? Whether rough or gentle, rape or love-making, it shall always end with you being held closely by me.

What happens if potty comes accidentally? *Mmmh, please baby, do not poop in my mouth. We will know when we are ready for that (I hope never!).* His sentiments entirely, as he confirmed...

I laughed out loud when I read this – another boundary to be inscribed in our Declaration, with amendments.

***

You are constantly on my mind. It's crazy, while dreaming, reading, working, there's John. I hope I will not drown you with my hunger for you and the love I will share you with.
Later, my sweet love; no solitude just now.

Thanks for letting me know, Baby! Frankly, the best time to write is when all is quiet and solitude abounds – don't stress about it. Enjoy offering hospitality and if nothing comes tonight my time, something good will be in my inbox sometime later.

My sweet love!

I wish we could Skype. I miss your face and voice (I will wait for the phone call tonight!). John and Lorraine sounds very good and correct. It's dawning on me, more and more, that I have declared to myself that you are the man for me. It feels so comfortable, like this is what I have been waiting for, for a very long time!

I love you!

My baby! Absorb the thought, recall everything that has been shared between us these past three weeks and recognize that we must take care to let 'life' and living reality catch up with our thoughts and dreams. This means taking care of each other's desires and frailties!

I need you desperately, in thoughts and action. (I'm becoming a little afraid that our desperation for each other might turn into an unfulfilled reality; I freeze. You must be patient with John!)

I am afraid too, John, but we will have to live it to know. I am totally committed to a pornographic life with you and pray and want it to work out.

For that to work, we should be stable emotionally. I would like to go on dates with you initially, to test myself and ourselves. We should be able to talk about other issues besides our pornographic lives, though I suppose it could

take up most of our time. Seriously, I want us to
work out, desperately so!
I am totally in love with you!

That's a very interesting idea: 'to go on dates'. The first weekend we will be together most of the time anyway, though I will have to get to Bintumani at some point on Saturday. That evening though, we are going to a quiet restaurant to eat, talk, plan and dream.

And I am totally in love with you too!

I want to savour you completely, John. My
totally new comprehension of this lifestyle and
its gloriousness is overwhelming, to say the least
(overwhelmingly welcomed, of course). I want to
know you, feel you, sense you, breathe you, and
much more. I love feeling! I have met my mate.
You complete me yet you scare me at the same
time, John. We are made of our environments
and sometimes, have chosen our unforeseen
journeys along our paths. We have fears
stemming from our earlier circumstances. I hate
that you are still grappling with yours. It's sad. I
understand your pain yet I do not. I know you
will understand that phrase. I want to help, if
you are ever ready. I had one of the most terrible
childhoods I could think imaginable (no, no
fucking and no poverty! Worse!). Maybe it
affected me (I really think it did. I do not know
how exactly. I am a sexual deviant for heaven's

sake! I must have been affected. One day, when you and I have calmed and sorted and aligned our parameters, when I can let go at my will, I want to tell you, everything and you will be the first. I want you to be the first that I tell.

I love the feeling of being yours.

This is good, Lorraine!

'I want to tell you everything and you will be the first. I want you to be the first that I tell'.

I so want that too. When you start talking and recounting all that happened, I will know that you have reached a point of emotional confidence both within yourself and with me. This will be a milestone to look forward to.

Just believe it; you are mine, all mine, exclusively mine in all things pure and depraved...

Love and more!

Look at what you sent me earlier; those questions too. How can I have found you? How can you be, after all my years, the one that fits with all my dreams and aspirations so perfectly! Not only are you a beautiful looking woman but you are simply 'hot'. As I told you, the manager at Bintumani used that very word when I told him that "we were getting to know each other!" Your face, your lips, your eyes, your smile, your laugh. Then to illustrate the *Perfection*... you send me these questions which I replied to yesterday (your time), but let me reply again, differently:

Will you let me watch porn when I want to? This we have settled. Your watching is our watching, How could it be otherwise? This is part of our essence.

Will you put your cock into me even when asleep? It is a delight that I can picture in my mind. The gentle approach is to make my cock wet and your cunt wet, with spit and fingers, then slip in from behind, on our sides. But sometimes, the rougher way shall take place. I will still make you wet quietly. Then, with you lying to one side, I shall roll you on your back, push your legs apart and as you wake slightly, will fill your cunt with my cock and give you the hundred thrusts session...

Will you sit on my face and threaten to go potty on my face? Sit on your face – certainly. I shall also play the word game, threatening to shit on to your face and into your mouth, 'you disgusting pig', but would never actually do it.

Will you spit in my mouth? You can rely on this happening, time and again. Where sometimes your nose shall be held, at others I shall simply tell you to "open your fucking mouth" and, if you refuse, I shall slap you and, if you still refuse, I shall slap you even harder until you comply. Then I shall spit and spit again.

Will you stick a dildo in my pussy while you fuck my ass? Interesting. I would have thought it would have been the other way around but either is a certainty at the right time, especially given your pictures with the dildo inserted accordingly!

Will you let me love you? I beg and plead for that, in its totality!

Will you shove your cock deep down my throat and choke me at the same time? There's going to be a certain pleasure, a vicious pleasure, a sort of raping feel to it; you choking and resisting, naturally, as you gag, me letting you breathe (the rapist having

197

momentary sympathy for his victim), then shoving in again, deep into your throat until you gag and almost vomit.

Will you shove your cock deep in my ass? You are such a slut that when we did it, you finally impaled yourself deeper and deeper on to my cock, shoving against me, you beautifully disgusting fucker, with the porno appetite of a dirty whore.

Will you please rape me unannounced? Roughly and savagely? Please? There is no question here, none at all. It shall be done and when the brutality is over and you are whimpering with a mixture of pain and pleasure... *Will you promise to hold me tight after after the ordeal?* Yes, I will hold and cherish the body I have just abused and with which I have amused myself, but (and this is important) for her ultimate pleasure, Lorraine, my twisted cunt.

If all this is not *perfection* in and from the woman of my dreams, what on earth is?

Then again:

You are my sophisticated gentleman who will torture me too and I absolutely love it! Torture me, my male whore! These are phenomenal statements. Rich men would pay millions to have a woman devoted to and surrendered to them as you have begged to be devoted to me and have declared your surrender to me.

In all this deeply sensual, erotic beauty, how can I possibly even be tempted to betray my Lorraine? She is everything I could wish for in a woman. This as has been stated many times. She is already *all* women to me. A good image of what you capture for your John, you have already shared. Let me remind you. The picture was of a sultry Italian-looking woman with sultry breasts and legs to match. The words were almost intoxicating:

Be the good girl he loves.

Be the bad girl he desires.

Be the naughty girls he lusts.

Be the lady her worships.

As we have both agreed several times, this is only the beginning. We have so, so much more to explore. Let it be so.

Meanwhile, let's agree on a safe word; it's going to be needed.

I have so much love for you, Lorraine, it is bursting out of me!

We will agree on a safe word when we have a sit down on Saturday evening. We have so much to talk about, sweetie!

I will try to reply to all the exquisite mails you sent me.

Friday cannot get here fast enough!

You did not tell me your arrival time.

Always wet for you!

Arrival time, 21.55.

Enjoy taking your time to write replies; savour the process (like we savour the prospect of wet, lovely sex, kissing and more).

I long to be with you!

I crave for you aggressively!

27.

I do not want to fear you cheating on me, I am going to leave it at that and we will just have to prove to each other, there's no other way. My baby, I can't stand the thought of that possibility. You have far more chances to cheat on me, gorgeous looking young woman! In a way (in a small way, watching porn without me is cheating). But you know what I mean. I have exposed my heart to you completely, and I want to feel and trust in that undying love and devotion from you. I need that badly. I know I'm getting it from you, except when we wobble very slightly. I love good quality porn, you idiot, but only as a shared experience!

My Savage!
You got me right! I have never been able to express. I almost gave up on this lifestyle because of so much selfishness that's why they say that you should be sure and stable emotionally, understanding boundaries and rules and respecting them. We are still working on that. That's why I keep saying that now, our living must catch up with our ideas these past three weeks or so. It will be done so long as we are caring of each other and of ourselves, for each other.

Yes, it's been a journey, torturous month indeed but I am grateful because through the thorns we have been able to emerge to our true carnal sense. I am truly grateful for all the mails and erotic photos and videos that we have shared. It's been thrilling! This is a statement of such beauty, Lorraine. It is also true!

...but I want my Savage back! Yes you are my sophisticated gentleman who tortures me and I absolutely love it! Torture me, my male whore! I am so excited for us! The wishes of my cunt-bitch shall be fulfilled; at times slowly, at others with almost vicious enthusiasm but ultimately, always controllable... Which begs the question (again) of a 'safe word'. We need one! Suggestions? (but not one you've used before). I have never had one because I have never reached this height of experience and potential mutual understanding. In my previous relationship, she told me of the experiences she'd had, when first we met: being tied down and beaten; being tied upside down to an upright ladder and abused; having a threesome. These are all things I yearned to do with her but was never given the opportunity and never felt the confidence to initiate matters. This is the essential contrast and illustration of how much further I have been able to come with you in this – what you call – the alternative 'lifestyle', wonderful Lorraine!

Please let's make it work! It's good for both of us! It's good for both of us. That's an understatement – a British characteristic – no bad thing in itself and I understand it in the way you have used it. The following is a word I do not normally use but in this case, in our case, the word 'awesome' is actually correct. If we manage to get our living to catch up with our thoughts, and move forward in the same way, our relationship, our partnership, our love, will indeed be 'awesome'!

Lorraine, my woman!

You have used the phrase 'this lifestyle' a couple of times recently. I've never thought of it and us in this way but you have introduced a concept – an idea – that embraces an entire universe. Can you therefore give me a definition – a description – of what you mean by 'this lifestyle'? This will help me with my total understanding of you and us.

Love and crazy dreams!

Well, to me 'this lifestyle' means, being in a relationship that is both open, in this case between John and Lorraine (and whatever delights they would like included, when agreed and very calm but very horny).

It sounds and feels (deliciously) savage, but it's very delicate in so many ways. It's still a taboo. It's a lifestyle against the norm. It's erotic! Exotic! Beastly! Decadent and we love it! We are not normal and we love it because we are so!

I don't know if I have answered or swayed from the question. Let me know, my hungry man!

This is perfect (that word again) but the specific word that stands out – and they are all applicable, exciting and correct – is 'taboo'! Excellent!

You exude a deep-seated sensuality that I recognized soon after seeing then speaking to you. You are not only my walking cunt but my walking, dripping cunt! That is what you exude; literally, cunt juices and metaphorically, walking ("take me I'm yours John") sex. I have complimented you on your walk, often and this is why.

Thank you, my Man!
I will drip more juices (more for you to fill your mouth with when I straddle your face). I will drip more cunt juices when I have you back!

Will you let me tear your clothes off once we get home immediately this Friday?

I'd better wear old clothes then, including the shirt I spoke of, that you were to wear.

What a good idea. I suspect now, that I shall do so. You see! You have the ideas (generally) and I follow. That's not to say that I don't have ideas but you are the primary source. You are also my primary source to the secrets and taboos in an open (Lorraine and John) relationship. I can't wait to start what will be a series of conversations. I also can't wait for you to start ripping my shirt off (literally) and dripping your cunt juices over my face and definitely, into my gaping mouth (actually)... I am your man in all things gentle and taboo.

No!

I want to see my dressed gentleman sauntering into arrivals. I promise not to tear them but I will definitely get you off them in seconds! We will get a good quiet place for ripping and oh so sweet torture sins. Do you agree?

Yes, we have so much to talk about and rediscovering each other emotionally and definitely, physically. I am on a constant wet drip since you left the country. My legs will reach for your neck to embrace the long lost dangerously loved tongue. You are amazing with your mouth as you are with every other part of your body. Oh, and my pussy has healed beautifully. It seems to get stronger!

I shaved last night because I had a doctor's appointment this morning (purely routine). I feel like a second hand car, getting my bits serviced. I will not shave again so that when I arrive, my face will be suitably designer-stubble rough.

I love you so much! My pornographic king!

My baby! I sense the need for endless analysis is waning, in that we have covered so, so much, That's OK because we need to move from understanding in principle to understanding and living in practice. That's not to say that you shouldn't write thoughts if inspired to do so. That's also not to say that you shouldn't identify other videos, or pictures that capture things you want done or applied to you or on you by me.

Meanwhile, I said I would add amendments to our declaration but have had no time (no solitude) to do so. I would like to though and to maintain it as a living document.

I love and desire you so very much, Lorraine, and I shall show you when again we are staring, touching, ripping and fucking each other. Practice your dripping because I need an awful lot of it, in my mouth so that I can taste and taste again, before swallowing some and bringing a share back to your delicious mouth and tongue.

I agree. I am anxiously waiting for you so we could start our pornographic lives.

I will write to you till you are back home safely. I love reading from you. You are a great writer! I loved your reactions after I send you photos, videos and erotic mails. I am constantly thinking of what else to show you, so no worries. They will keep coming even when you are back. Promise me that you will not stop writing to me when you are back. I am addicted to these mails.

Having a declaration document is really a good idea. Please show it me when you are finished editing but take your time.

I will drip for you my baby. I am ready to be savoured by you and I you!

28.

I am anxiously waiting for you so we can start our pornographic lives! *You are a truly amazing porno priestess! Even to abbreviate the word is slutty!*

I am constantly thinking of what else to show you, so no worries. They will keep coming, even when you are back. *Ah this is too much in that it is fantastic that you want to go on and on and on in this genre.*

Having a declaration document is really a good idea. Please show it to me when you are finished editing but take your time. *With luck, certainly tomorrow, when the house will be empty.*

Okay, baby, but I want red hot pain...

My dearest fucker, you shall receive as much 'red hot pain' as you desire. As I will not feel your pain you must be the judge of how much you can accept. What I can feel is your pleasure through your reactions; the body and skin quivering, your voice faltering, your screams echoing throughout your apartment or wherever else these opportunities might present themselves.

You make me want to be bad! I can honestly tell you that I have never been excited about what lies ahead as I am now. I have had these opportunities and as you pointed out (I didn't think of it until later), I never found the perfect fit before but now I feel ready! And even when very comfortable, in my previous situation, I was there and the first emotions that I would have would be fear (yes, even after being the initiator; yes, most times), hatred, woken up anger but mostly, hatred for him and now, after I have grown up a tiny bit, I realise why it was wrong in the first place, like with your previous (reversed).

I hate to say it but I behaved like her, apart from the rendezvous that was there with other girls, we barely had a sex life. I could not bring myself to even dare savour the moment, so I found a way to absolutely not have sex with him. I felt terrible but I just couldn't do it. He made me feel like I could scream if he touched me. I did occasionally. The reason I am telling you all this is because I have found you, I have found someone who finally makes sense for me with my (I used to think I was emotionally ill) pornographically infused head. You did not push me, I am this being and I have found a person: you, John! You complete the picture of 'what to have a pornographic partner' means. You describe in rich clear words what you love

and care about in being a beast, a beast that literally makes me wet even from your mail!
We are going to have fun!

'I used to think I was emotionally ill (with my) pornographic infused head... I am this being...'
This is such a revealing message. -Thanks for sharing. The bedrock of our pornographic as well as genuine love is the sex between you and me. I can't think of a moment that I would not want to touch you and sleep with you and I cannot think of a more awful situation than you turning against the idea of sex with me, like with your previous man. From that starting point, your words above – *you thought you were ill* – sick in the head. As we have both admitted, I have helped you to uncover the real you, the beautifully slutty you, the exquisite BDSM you. In turn, I have found the total partner in you. Your sick mind (according to others) is matched by my sick mind (for those judgmental types). We are as one, you and I. Prepare yourself!

And indeed, we *are* going to have fun, in the context of friendship, laughter and love. Just have your lighter and /or matches always available!

I will have my matches, my love! I hope we will be on our own!
We are one, you and I, baby. We finally can enjoy and explore our other selves without judgment. I am scared that it's too perfect. Are you?
I want you in me right now!

My love! The idea of being scared, the possibility of a massive anti-climax (excuse the pun) has crossed my mind; that's only natural. But with all that has been revealed between us and from us these past weeks, I can assure you that I feel very confident emotionally and therefore, even if I am exhausted after twenty-four hours of moving through the air by plane and through two airports (by foot), the strongest muscle in (everybody's) body – the tongue – will flash its desire into your cunt and asshole, without question. In any case, apart from my tongue, my cock yearns for your hands, your mouth, your cunt and your asshole, though the order of penetration (and / or manipulation) shall be determined by the spirit of the moment.

I love you dearly, Lorraine!

I love you passionately, my erotic woman!

I love you pornographically, my dripping walking cunt!

John! I feel too confident. For once in my life, I am ready to let go, rather than run like a little puss. I am putting all my trust in you, John Evans; my chosen lover, my chosen torturer. When we sit down, we will talk about everything, then we can start living. I just wish it was not in this country; that's my only hiccup.

When you get home, you tell me if you would want a shower first (I bet! Or not!) food or any beverage, or if you would prefer my preference, to be in bed in two seconds after we alight from the taxi. You choose.

I feel too confident. We talk on Saturday p.m. in a quiet restaurant... have you chosen it?

I just wish it was not in this country; that's my only hiccup. The alternative possibilities will take time and care but I have been thinking about this a lot. -We shall discuss because I need to get all aspects of my own family stuff sorted out as well. That will then allow for other possibilities – for you and me, geographically.

...would prefer my preference, to be in bed in two seconds... My choice is simple. If the flights are all OK, I will have showered in Brussels. I will still smell of residual perspiration from the plane but if you can take that dirty aspect of your man, then let's get to bed in two seconds flat! If my flight to Brussels is delayed and I have no opportunity to shower, I shall be even closer to being a beast man in smell as, in any case, a cleaner version of the same beast, if all flights run smoothly. In short, no food or drink will be needed. Just to drink your cunt juices and if available, your piss.

Beast smell or your usual heavenly smell, I will still take you, with all the passion my body could handle. Never have I ever wanted a body so much! Yours, baby, I worship it!
Cunt juices will be served with relish.

I begin to be lost for words! We are both excited in the extreme, with a tinge of fear that it seems too perfect to be believed, which it is already in words and dreams. As before, all we have to do is to turn the whole idea of us into an exquisite love and pornographic reality. My heart is yours, baby. After what we have been through from the first meeting till my departure, it is a miracle as well as a triumph for us to have reached this glorious moment; the few days till we are embraced in our universe, in our totality.

29.

I am like a little child now. I am hoping that there will be more mail waiting for me in the morning; that you have not exhausted your days quota (writing to me). I always look forward to your mails. They make my day! Absolutely!

I love you so much. Stay positive. Things will work out.

My loved gentle, savage beast!

I love you like I have never been able to before. It is a dream that I have met you. It is even more of a dream that you are letting me flourish in my longed for but never truly fulfilled, 'alternative lifestyle'.

Thank you so much!

You sleep and I shall write once more later tonight (my time).

Okay, my love. Stay in that great erotic space till we see each other. I cannot lose you. In any sense, I have found a Male Me! And I love him!

Goodnight, sweetie.

I'm bouncing between the cooker and my bedroom! I shall never stray from our erotic space. Sometimes it will be under the surface; at others, completely exposed but always, always there.

I know how you feel about receiving e-mails and feeling disappointed when they are not there. I have precisely the same feeling and fear.

Another perfect phrase: 'I have found a Male Me!' You most certainly have.

Oh, I forgot to tell you, I sent my friend your photo (sorry) and the first thing that she said finally... 'Hahaaa'! she thinks you are hot! I totally agree!

Is she saying HOT to please you or does she mean it? Either way, I look forward to meeting your best friends someday (though I doubt in Russia).

No! My friends and I are very honest with each other. They hated my ex and what he had done to me and how miserable I was. They kept bugging me to leave him, so when Marina is approving (and she has an opinion about everything), I believe her. And why in god's name do you doubt when people think you are hot? Don't be silly.

Noted. I shall try not to 'be silly' again!

Hi, sweetie. I meant to reply earlier but there's been some commotion at home with Alice and her man, so I had to sit with them. She just left for work and then I got a Skype call from my New Zealand friend in Addis. I've been feeling guilty but she understood. She asked me about you - so curious! She says she hopes to meet you. Those two are what I could call my best friends in the whole world.

I will go back to our erotic mails after I finish with some chores.

Two more days? My pussy is desperate for you!

I am trying to keep calm about only two days left! It's ten degrees below zero here and will be minus twenty tomorrow. I need the warmth of Freetown's heat and the heat of. your body and mind!

Does any friend know of your dark side, the lifestyle you seek to pursue? Just trying to gain more understanding of where the boundaries are.

No! And I would not want to share it at all. Please, John!

I did that with the girl I fell out with; our neighbour. She has a big mouth, so I am sure she has shared but I don't care about that. This is our world, baby. You tell people, the next would be my family! That's how it works in this stupid country (forgive me, I get testy about how Freetown people behave). We will have to spend more time fucking so I can forget about living in this country. I hate it!

This hatred of her county was something John did not really understand. It had its challenges, certainly. It had its attractions too. One was the relaxed attitude to the 'man-woman' or, indeed, 'woman-man' thing. Maybe it had something to do with the climate; often very humid and certainly very hot at the appropriate time of year and with torrential – really torrential – rain at other times. When looking on to the Atlantic from his sitting-room window, sometimes it was crystal clear, with the sea simply shimmering. At other times, the wall of grey came rolling in, the downpour started and from that moment till it stopped, there was no view, not even of the shore line, which was, as the crow flies, no more than about five hundred yards away.

Then she was moved to write about boundaries; clearly another raw nerve touched.
1. No sharing about our deep secrets with anyone. That would upset me very much.
2. No staring at my friends when you meet them (Freetown life again). I see it every day with my friends, seeing someone's man staring and he obviously wanting her. And the story sticks and becomes a fact. It is so annoying and

embarrassing. Add that to our declaration if you agree.

I agree completely on both counts; it shall be done. Now get back to the second and last messages – that is, re-enter our world.

He simply couldn't get enough of it. He was behaving like a child, wanting more of his favourite toy; no pun intended in that toys were to feature when he brought back the package, ordered through Amazon, while they were still optimistic, before their most recent bust-up, for which the intervening month had seen this array of what purported to be healing messages of emotion and porn.

My beast partner and my woman!

This world of ours – this lifestyle that you speak of – that we knew, almost immediately but launched into it clumsily and with potentially disastrous consequences, has re-emerged as a world full of love, desire and promise. At its heart is the idea that we have both conceded to in so many words, and at so many times, of surrender, total and complete surrender. That's not just the idea of you allowing me to administer BDSM on you and indeed, into you but a more telling surrender. The surrender is one of complete belief. You are now telling me of your complete belief in me, in that I am the male version of you. You must therefore concede to the fact that you are the female version of me. In so declaring, we are so perfectly matched (that 'perfect' word again) because we lust and hunger for the same things in each other. This means first and foremost, that we have a complete longing and trust in each other;

that nothing can shake us apart because neither of us will do anything knowingly to threaten what we have. But, if ever either of us does something or says something that could cause the other discomfort or pain, we must not, repeat not, withdraw into ourselves or go into a fury and binge session(s). We must speak in the context of that total and fundamental trust in each other.

You have already confessed to your surrender to me and I am now declaring the same to you. I treasure my heart. I want it protected but I want you – my love – to do the protecting!

I know you are a different person to the one I left. I have all the emails to prove it! You are a fantastic and courageous woman. I love that aspect of you. But I love the dirty and depraved side of you as well, such as your willingness to expose your body, and indeed your mind, to the thrill of physical surrender and all that implies in a sound and solid BDSM relationship. Just one small part of our total lifestyle to come! For an example, see the second message.

My heart is yours, baby! My body is yours, baby! My entire being is yours, baby! Take care of it for me as I shall take care of your heart, your body and your entire being.

Love and more,

John.

My beast man!

I will never knowingly hurt you and I know you wouldn't hurt me either, knowingly. We are both scared of the 'what ifs', I am trying so much not to give it any thought. I have surrendered to you completely, John, as you have declared your dedication to me. I don't want to ever hurt you.

I am an emotional person (besides sexual) and like you wrote the other day '...if I sense some exclusion I will shut down...' I understand you completely. Because baby, that is me. Everyone who knows me knows that I shut down too often. I don't want to do that with you, at all! Would it even last long enough? I don't know. The reason why I did not want to lose you after our last horror fight was because I knew I had not been able to know you enough - at all, actually! But I knew, deep in my heart, that you were a good person and you were the match to everything that I was looking for in a man and now you have proven to me that there's even much more and it proves that my instincts were right after all.

What I am trying to say here is I am so happy and grateful that I got you back! (I have promised myself and written a long letter to myself.) I will not share you with another woman. My radar on cheating is always on high alert (it comes with my history of choosing bad men). I will walk out of the relationship calmly and with no problems. I have promised myself that.

We will share with another person(s) when we are ready and even then, we have to understand the rules (you will learn with time that rules are what makes it or break it).

That was not a threat and I don't want you to think so. That's why we need more quiet dates, so we could learn more about each other and what pushes our buttons. I am really looking forward to that.

Another woman – never. What need of it. I now have you, my total woman! A threesome, yes, but only and I mean only at your instigation. You shall arrange (one of your boundary messages has already presented the rules, part of the forthcoming amendments to our declaration will confirm.

Thank you for declaring that, Baby! That is my biggest fear. A fear that literally paralyses my life. I don't ever want to be in that horrible space again. I am so glad you took the initiative to draft our declaration. It will be there to remind us of our promises to each other.

You also have expressed a desire (in conversation) to have three woman doing wicked things to themselves and possibly us, but again, this is entirely up to you and at your gift, your instigation.

Baby! When the time feels right, it will happen. I want it to happen but I want it to be with women that will enjoy the moment with us. It will take some time but I will always try to come up with juicy surprises for you. Making you and us happy and excited is one of my top priorities.

The primary agenda is what I can do to you and with you and what we can do to and with each other! Please understand that! What you must understand also is that, for all the obvious pornographic reasons, I am your partner in all such exploration and fun. What you must also understand, yet again, is that you are so, so important to me, so treasured as a woman – a complete woman – that to threaten such a love and partnership is fucking unthinkable!

At last! You will be here, we will have no barred or censored conversation (promise me that). I promise you to be fully open to you. That is after our fucking and you having a bit of food and rest.

30.

Designer stubble for my arrival? Yes or no?

In other words, I need to know if you want your inner thighs to be scratched a little as I attack your cunt. I need to know if you want to feel my growth on your breasts and nipples as I kiss and suck hard. I need to know if your mouth and face are willing to accept that roughness?

I want your stubby facial hair to scratch my inner thighs and pussy and when I kiss you. I love how you look with a few days growth of beard; sexy and you being rough symbolizes for me my torturer, the torture that I love!

I am accepting, inviting and welcoming your stubble growth. Because I love it!

'...your breasts and nipples as I suck kiss and suck hard'. Oh, you give me delicious thoughts through your writing, the way you write is fantastic.

We are on, baby!

'We are on' indeed, baby, and my cock rises at the prospect; my juices I keep for you! My torture techniques are yet to be revealed and explored; by both of us, you delicious cunt!

Mmmh, torture techniques are yet to be revealed! There's a wet spot in my panties now!

You know what? When I put up the advertisement on craigslist, it was more out of boredom and slight curiosity, that maybe there was someone who would understand me. Was I not given what I was looking for (but did not expect) and so much more? This has to work!

Keep those juices for my hungry open mouth!

I proudly call you my man, my partner!

Good girl and thank you!

When being introduced, will you refer to me as your boyfriend or your partner?

I have been using the boring title 'boyfriend', I prefer 'my partner' (has more depth). I will start using that title.

John, my Partner!

Excellent answer! I am your partner and you are my partner. Boyfriends and girlfriends come and go but an emotional partnership conveys to the outside world an enduring commitment.

Absolutely! My loving man!

My love, we have so much to talk about, on so many levels. On all levels, loving, living and lusting for each other, we shall take our time...

We will take our time, with patience and sometimes greedily impatient to rip clothes off each other!

***

His impatience knew no bounds. He sent her a picture of a red candle, its wax dripping on to her uptight nipple, simply teasing the rest of her breast. The caption read 'A sample of what you're going to get when the moment is right'.

Yes, yes, yes! My devious man! I should be tied down when you drip hot candle wax on me; mmmh, my skin is tingling thinking of it!
I want this really badly! I am going to melt a little bit of wax on myself and test how it will feel but it's not same as if you poured wax on me, especially if you are fully dressed and I am naked and helpless because I have been tethered by wrists and ankles.

Was there any wonder that he was now becoming completely besotted with her? To his credit, this was also tempered by a modicum of care for the recipient of such pleasure, such torture, such welcomed taboo.

According to my reading, the candle should be wide (fat) so that the wax can gather before being poured. If it's a narrow (thin) candle, then the wax is too immediately burnt, too hot. Secondly, the wax should be poured from an elevated position, so that fractional cooling, through the air, is achieved. But don't be worried; it'll still be fucking hot for Lorraine! Finally, your gentleman torturer is to test the wax on his wrist first. If he can take it, so can she. If it hurts your torturer but he can still cope with the heat, it shall be poured, without mercy, as outlined above, in words and pictures. Enjoy the prospect of torture to come! I am your man in this and everything else.

Oh, you are so sweet! You did some research! I like that and I like that you care. Test it and let me know but trust me, honey. I am not afraid of any kind of pain (sensual pain) when our clothes are off. Always remember that.
I am so ready, sweetheart.

Again, he couldn't believe what he was reading. She wanted everything and more. Torture, in the form of hot wax being dripped upon her delicate parts and other women, for her pleasure and his. It was a pornographic dream in a loving reality. The question then would be, if all this is in the context of love, how can it be pornographic? After all, *Lady Chatterley's Lover* was challenged in the English courts, in essence, as being pornographic and therefore, not worthy of publication. The challenge failed: something to do with recognizing the genuine emotional context of the lover's anguish for his own unrequited emotion which at times, translated itself into full descriptions of sexual desire and rare accomplishment.

They managed to speak again...

You, my beauty, are thus an openly self-confessed masochist. Pain through hot wax, pain through a whip, pain through a very strong hand.

I'm in disbelief; rapturous disbelief not only because of your declaration (pain) but also, if you are a masochist, my god, I must be a sadist, deriving sexual, erotic and pornographic pleasure from inflicting sensual pain upon you. This is becoming deliriously overwhelming!

Is that what I am? A masochist? I gladly confess it! And yes, you are a sadist! I love it that you are, my sexy sadist! Did you never consider this before, this lifestyle? You have written about it pornographically, deliciously so.

Never have I considered this before as a 'living' part of me. Writing of it is one thing but living the reality? I never dreamed that I would end up with a person who would present it to me in life. Again: yes in imagination and again, never thinking that it would actually be possible.

Which brings the question up; besides your new love for BDSM, what else do you like apart from pissing and periods, please let me in.

At this moment, I really cannot think. Let's explore in conversation and again to repeat, I never thought about three women enjoying themselves and possibly us. I never thought about shemales and sucking their cocks (another gem you slipped into one of our recent rare telephone conversation). You are much better at initiating than me so let your clever ideas flow. I shall respond but if additional thoughts do appear (like the candles), I will certainly share with my whore woman; my fucking masochist, my candle singed cunt!

It's very hard to believe, yet I believe you. Your erotic books had me fooled (got me raving jealous too). You expressed your passion and knowledge so perfectly. If I did not know you and I got your books, I would masturbate and cum to your books so many times; only I was fucking jealous!

Well, now! It's in your life, sweetheart, and don't you think otherwise anymore. I want to be fucked in all ways by you, trying out our fantasies and finding new ones.

Do not worry thinking about new fantasies. We have plenty to last us some time. We will have fun with ourselves for some time. I think it's best with what we have gone through. We definitely will have conversations about all this once you are here and maybe you will tell me what you think about a shemale choking you with her cock!

I am your candle singed cunt!
I fucking adore you!

Thank you for trusting me, believing in me and fighting to get me back into your life. We have a long and lovely road ahead of us. I cannot wait to start on this journey with you, sweetheart! My perfect pornographic partner!

My baby, agreed! Just to let you know that my adrenalin is starting to flow and I'm not even travelling till tomorrow. I'm almost nervous – interesting.

You are nervous as I am, baby! We are meeting again but we know that this time, it is different, it definitely is! Travel safe, my honey. I will be there when you come from arrivals!

Meanwhile, scented candles often carry chemicals than can cause temporary skin irritation beyond the purity of sensual pain. That's why the two fat white candles are unscented. Scented candles from China are recommended to be avoided, particularly.

I have just returned from three stores; all red candles are scented so I have not touched them. In any case, if you are blindfolded (which you might be, unless you want to watch the administering of torture in its naked and frightening reality), what need of a specific colour?

Dream on, my love!

So funny! About the scented candles from China. Again, thank you for caring.

PS. I don't know if Alice will be here on Friday night. I hope not because it will mean her man will be here too. So, if the environment is a bit crowded, then I would rather not let them hear my screams of pleasure from being pussy-singed!

If we are not alone, all they shall hear is your occasional muffled laughter and groans of pleasure. If we find ourselves alone and the mood is right, after some conventional re-bonding sucking and fucking, I shall place a blanket or quilt over the dining table, tie you to it with legs and arms pulled apart, light the candle, let you see the flame flicker, talk dirty to you, use threatening language even, then proceed to let the wax drip, Drip, DRIP on to various parts of you.

But only and I mean only if all circumstances are correct for such an event. For example, that you are begging and I am on fire (metaphorically speaking).

Love to my burning slut!

We still have my room for lots of fucking! Hard and soft. I don't think this is the best environment for BDSM, especially not the dining area. First, the curtains are sheer; everyone sees

through our house all day and all night long.
Don't you worry, we have our weekend away. I
want to be completely comfortable and not worry
at all being found tied down or neighbours
having a field day watching intense porn (it's
nosey Freetown, after all)! No, this is not the best
environment for BDSM. I would not be
comfortable. I hope you understand but we have
plenty to explore before the weekend. It's not a
'no'. We are just pushing the dripping of wax to
the next coming weekend.

I love you, baby!

Clearly, my love, the circumstances are not correct, not propitious. In any case, I can torture you with my teeth... Relax! Waxing and whipping will come in good time and in good places.

Teeth torture sounds delicious!
Waxing?

Hot candle wax... I wanted a word that began with a 'w' to match whipping. Odd? Now to bed for the last time alone. Next time, I am deeply embedded in your cunt!

Not odd, just wondering. .

Oh, one day! I will be at the airport by eight
p.m., to meet you, hug you for a minute longer,
kiss and savour your mouth! Write to me when

you wake up. Sweet dreams about our future prospects. I totally adore you, John! Goodnight.

31.

My dearest Lorraine,

Here is my last gesture to us before I depart this place for the sanctity of your body; version 2 of our declaration. Sit quietly then read, read and read again. The original you already know. The amendments we have declared in so many ways while I have been away. In this concentrated form, they are very powerful!

Savour them. If more are required, they shall be revealed in time. If changes to the attached are needed, we shall agree them.

You have me, Lorraine; the entirety of my mind, heart and body, including my cock and my balls; all three of which need your attention, badly!

Love and so much deviously more!

To me, Lorraine, this is the epitome of wickedness! It is delicious in its duality of symbolism; good and wicked (which means even better). In a curious way, it captures you and me. This is the beginning of the extremes we both seek to explore with each other's help, care and love. I love you to the point of madness; a good madness, a creative madness but one where I am willing to let myself go and lay myself and my heart at the mercy of one Lorraine Cooper. Do you understand this? I am saying to you what you are increasingly saying to me. You want the totality of me and my welcome of you, in all your sublime, erotic, sensual and pornographic ambitions. Let me tell you that, in such matters (and more besides), you have found the ideal partner. How do I know? Because we have come though fire to get to this point. When I finally get back to you, all the necessary healing will be behind us. We shall re-combine with a month of reconstruction 'in the bag'. Love and porn, your man whore!

To John: I promise to take care of you.

I am letting myself go and trusting you to always be there, no walking out on each other, no threats, no disrespect for each other, to always listen and empathize, sympathize, be patient.

I promise to work on my weak points and harder on being your pornographic priestess.

Reading your sentiments about your feelings about me makes me feel very grateful, special and beautiful, thank you, my whore. You have the totality of me.

We will be fine, I believe that. I cannot wait to have you back, back in my life and bed!

I have found my perfect man; let's be good to each other.

First Amendment

1. Health safety at all times when and if we indulge in a threesome. You cannot finger her and finger me with the same hands. That is one of my greatest fears.

2. We are not to pick prostitutes, friends or anyone familiar to us.

3. You cannot exchange numbers or anything personal with any of the girls.
4. The girl/s cannot ever sleep over! When done, a cab should be arranged for her/them.
5. I am not always in a mood for a threesome and would appreciate if John understood that.
6. I would prefer if we never had girls in either of our homes.

Second Amendment
7. Will you let me watch porn when I want to? YES!
8. Will you put your cock into me even when asleep? YES!
9. Will you sit on my face and threaten to go potty on my face? YES!
10. Will you spit in my mouth? YES!
11. Will you stick a dildo in my pussy while you fuck my ass? YES!
12. Will you let me love you? YES!
13. Will you shove your cock deep down my throat and chock me at the same time? YES!
14. Will you shove your cock deep in my ass? YES!
15. Will you please rape me un-announced? Roughly and savagely? Please? YES!

16. Will you promise to hold me tight after the ordeal? YES!

Third Amendment

17. I should be tied down when you drip hot candle wax on me.
18. I want this torture really badly!

Fourth Amendment

19. No sharing about our deep secrets with anyone; that would upset me very much.
20. No staring at my friends when you meet them (Freetown life again). I see it every day with my friends saying someone's man was staring at her and he must have wanted her. And the story sticks and becomes a fact.

Fifth amendment

21. Our 'lifestyle': being in a relationship that is both open, in this case between John and Lorraine (and whatever delights they would like included, when agreed and very calm but very horny). It sounds and feels (deliciously) savage but it is very delicate in so many ways. It is still a taboo; a lifestyle against the norm. It is erotic, exotic, beastly, decadent, and we love it!

22. We are not normal and we love it that that we are so!

Sixth Amendment
23. You, my beauty, are an openly self-confessed masochist! Pain through hot wax; pain through a whip, pain through a very strong hand.
24. If you are a masochist, I must be a sadist; deriving sexual, erotic and pornographic pleasure from inflicting sensual pain upon you.

Seventh Amendment
25. I want to be fucked in all ways by you, trying out our fantasies and finding new ones.

My sweet, beautiful John!

I have read and re-read and I don't have a change of mind on any of them. I am glad you came up with the idea and to have the option of adding more is also great. You have me too, my sweetheart, including my hot pulsating pussy that needs your attention terribly!

Twenty-four hours later and I will have you in my arms and later, embedded in me with you impaling me with your phenomenal manhood!

***

It is sad to leave the family but joyous to come to you!

I am so glad you are coming to me.

I am coming to you in more ways than just coming to you and (playfully), coming over your face and mouth must be on our fucking agenda. I simply cannot wait any longer. I need you Lorraine, very, very much!

32.

Lorraine, my beast woman!

No wonder you went berserk with me when you did! From the moment you started reading the first book, you were jealous (your admission)! Each book reinforced your worst fears. The word 'manipulation' entered the scene, often. From the first triggering of your jealously (your mistrust in the man you were with), you sought (unwittingly perhaps) to prove that your fear – your accusation – was correct. In your mind, the threesome (that started well but went horribly wrong) vindicated your fear; that I was just another 'fuck-around' man, just like your most recent ex.

Now I understand you even more – thank the lord we have had this month to digest the nuances of our respective psychologies!

Gorgeous Lorraine! I wouldn't threaten us for the world. We have so much to live for, with and for each other! That's why our unfolding – or evolving declaration – is so important.

Love and terrific sex ambitions!

Your man!

My god! How can you understand me this much! (My goose pimples are sticking out!) This is the entire confusion. Exactly how I would have described that ordeal. Is it possible to love you even more?

I am so grateful for the time apart even though it has been an ordeal. I see you more clearly. I am appreciating you so much more. I want to show you how thankful I am to have you in my life with so much delicious wickedness! I want to see you more, I want to know you!

Thank you, my John!

How can you understand me this much? In short perhaps...

I'll take care of you *psychologically* if you take care of me *emotionally*. In that, I am stronger than you psychologically and you are stronger than me emotionally.

It's almost three p.m. (eleven p.m., your time) and I'm leaving for the airport now. In twenty-three hours (a long, long journey), I shall be in your arms and soon after, in your bed. My stubble shall be suitable in its roughness.

33.

She was there. If a dark, sultry, pale-skinned woman could blush, she did. The taxi, the ferry, the drive to Bintumani. They changed their location because her flat was besieged by friends. She talked incessantly, while groping his cock and massaging his balls through his jeans. She wanted to fit the conversation to their last month of writing. Everything had to catch up. It was a frenzy of schoolgirl joy and hot-woman passion,

They arrived, got into his apartment and strangely, after everything said and done, they 'made love' with such intensity and mutually expressed emotion. This was no dirt, no porn, no bad language; just deeply penetrating love-making. Inevitably, they were soon asleep. When they woke and before anything else happened, they were at it again, this time with more of the dark-side thrown in. Appetites had been whetted.

John needed to get all his stuff (and his mind) into order. He ordered a taxi for Lorraine. This was Saturday. He sorted out his business, clothes shopping and the like. They went out later and talked endlessly. Her imagination was fired up.

"Sweetie, write to me about this stuff, it's hot and now that we are together, it must be explored; you must share these beautifully wicked ideas with me!"

They slept again that night, still coming to terms with each other after a month – a very long and emotionally liberating month – apart. They went to their favourite Sunday brunch location in town. They parted company. It seemed illogical that they should not be together – that is, living together but his rational mind knew that care must still be taken, just in case.

***

He returned to work on Monday morning. The greetings were warm and heartfelt. It was good. He went home – not having opened his personal e-mail address all day; too much of a distraction, and found this in his in-box.

You come back from work and find me in a skimpy dress, reading a book. When I stand up to meet and kiss you because you look so handsome and hot, you give me a hard smarting slap on my face and grab my neck and roughly, push me down. I am trying to protest but you have your bag of tricks ready. With one hand still grasping my neck, you get the gag and roughly shove it down my throat. Before I know it, I am gagged, trussed up and you are now tearing the clothes with so much anger, I am scared and trembling and I don't know what is next. I can't talk, so I cannot plead for mercy. You fuck me in all holes the whole night.

No mercy for me: spit, piss, cum, deep throat, forcing your cock, balls, ass on my face while cursing me loudly.

I still want this, John. I want this and badly! I'm in heat for all this conquering stuff. Please...

...and you SHALL have it, without warning and without knowledge of how it will unfold because even I won't know until the spirit grabs my balls accordingly.

They spoke and as they did so, the spectre of Kate drifted into the conversation, a matter he thought he had expunged from their collective psyche.

And just in case you think I still hanker for you with Kate again (a slight suspicion in your voice just now), let me set this little matter to rest. What I would love to see again, is you entwined and being sucked by another woman and me sitting there fully clothed just watching – nothing but watching – even if you were embroiled with this woman who you do not like anymore, suitably twisted!

Do not mention Kate again. It makes my heart bleed every time you mention her and a future possibility. I am terribly hurt because I think you would want her again.

This was at the heart of so much recurring negativity, mistrust even. Kate was the focus of the original threesome, that which started beautifully and ended in acrimony and occasional violent outbursts, verbal sometimes and occasionally, physical. She was the other woman in the first chapter.

***

The second night Lorraine came to John's flat, she was staring out of the kitchen window. Her ass was inviting, he was horny so he fulfilled what he presumed to be a pleasure for her. He pushed her down on to the counter, her ass ready, undid her trousers, revealed her cunt and proceeded to fuck it and her. Her moans of pleasure could disguise nothing but that. The bread knife, with its serrated edge, lay on top of the chopping board. Suddenly she took it (to his shock) and placed the blade in her mouth (to his inexplicable excitement). Months after that incident, she sent him a question:

Why did a knife deep in my mouth thrill you?

It will need an email reply. My mind is now working on it subliminally, as I work.

Just finished working now! Must eat before anything else.

Of course, my love, replenish all the energy. You will need it tomorrow night! (Make sure it's only food that you will eat!) I am joking. I am in love with a man who makes me feel so complete and yet so incomplete. You cannot offer me more than us living together, which is exciting but that's not how reality rolls and I block it from my mind most times except when I let myself wander there. I get really scared because I love you very much! That's all.

This I understand (as you know). I just plead for patience and to move, step by step. The fact is, I love you very much too, and it grows.

I promise to be a little bit more patient.

This was at the heart of the emotional side. Where was this relationship going? He knew the potential of where it could go but having failed before and knowing her history, it required care and mutual understanding, as well as patience. His contract was only till August; the programme had still to be extended by two years (on the cards). He needed that first decision in place. By then, he reasoned (in a couple of months), their emotional selves would have caught up with their pornographic selves; the alternative lifestyle would be on solid foundations. Thus, once the contract extension was in place, they would be on solid 'lifestyle' foundations, they would move into an apartment together. With that achieved and the following two years of living, loving and fucking, they would know what the next step might be – so Lorraine's fears could be allayed.

34.

I'm still trying to think about the bread knife in your mouth. as my shoulders and upper back are screaming with the anguish of being on the keyboard all day. However:

1. It reflected your own desire to experience dangerous thrills, which thrilled me, knowing that I had met a woman who not only loved to be fucked, let alone 'taken', but the idea of you wanting genuine danger.

2. It conveyed a yearning for masochism; you wanted the idea of fear, a delicate side of the dark factor. I thrill at the idea of you wanting it.

3. Then there's the sense of torture – totally wicked – taboo even and therefore another level of pleasure for me to experience when seeing you fearing and suffering accordingly.

Oh, sweetie!
You convey it so beautifully and are so utterly correct! I remember that moment vividly. It was beautiful and I was feeling braver being around you and I wanted to show you my dark side and it turned me on a great deal by how you reacted, by pounding me and biting my neck while growling so sexily! A thrilling current has just run through my body! Mmmmmh...

We have so much to explore, my love, with our two deviant minds, we could never be bored.

***

Indeed they weren't. They behaved like depraved animals.

One other time, they were in the kitchen, she with her arms outstretched against the windowsill, leaning partially on the cool marble counter, he digging his cock deep into her cunt and her gasping for more and more.

He saw the bread knife on top of the microwave. While still thrusting and therefore keeping her mind on that fact, he was able to surprise her – stun her even – into her obvious pleasure in feeling the serrated edge of the blade being pulled across her shoulders. She screamed and begged for more. He withdrew from her cunt, gave himself space and pulled the blade right down her back; one side and then the other. He criss-crossed her ass cheeks. She then begged for more across her shoulders.

"More, John! Cut me, John! Let me feel the blade!"

He resisted cutting even in his heated state. Instead, he turned her round and repeated the cutting movements across one breast then the other, giving particular attention to each nipple. That generated suitable gasps.

"Fuck me again, John!"

He took her to the bathroom where she inclined over the sink but still able to see her upper body in the mirror. He had dashed into the bedroom to take his spare belt. He inserted himself deep into her cunt again, thrust after thrust with deliberation then whisked the belt, unbeknown to her, round her throat. She gasped again as he leaned back but keeping himself upright with the belt straining round her neck. He pulled and pounded, pulled and pounded until she came and as she whimpered, he exploded with his load firing deep into her. They were both completely done.

***

She kept talking about 'wanting pussy' and asking if he'd agree, subject to the condition that if anything happened it wouldn't be in his apartment. She put an ad into Craigslist. Replies came. She negotiated, arranged and on the appointed Friday night, Lorraine met the spare pussy at a nearby and suitably seedy hotel. She would text John if they clicked. An affirmative text came. He walked over to the place, found them and merged into their tight togetherness. He was strangely relaxed about the whole thing.

"Relax, John. Don't be tense. Don't spoil this for us!"

It was an annoying interjection because he felt completely at ease. Lorraine and the twenty-something girl both drank and drank some more. After about two hours of wine and tequilas (John had one beer), they agreed it was time to move. John rented the room, came back and encouraged them to move. He took them there. They looked at the place – fine – then Lorraine turned to John...

"We need to get some weed!"

They came back about twenty minutes later, lit started puffing and between puffs, peeled off their clothes. John did too. Once all were naked, they kissed wet kisses on each other's mouths, held each other in a triangle, then John withdrew, encouraging Lorraine to proceed with the conquest. She did, moving from the spare pussy's mouth, to her breast, then her cunt, slurping and enjoying. John then started kissing her as well; mouth, breasts then finding himself being pulled by Lorraine to have both their tongues lashing at her pussy.

"Get the condom! I want you to fuck her!"

With condom donned, Lorraine took his manhood and steered it into the guest's cunt. There was no subtlety, just hard fucking, with Lorraine stroking his balls and wanting him to go harder. Then they both realized that she had become limp, just lying there. Both stopped.

"Are you all right?" Lorraine asked her.

Before the answer came, the girl moved awkwardly to the toilet, kneeled and started vomiting. After a bit, she admitted to "having drunk too much". She came back, lay down and within seconds, was sound asleep. John and Lorraine looked at each other, agreed to pull the covers over her, leave the agreed payment on the bedside table, near her quietly breathing mouth, tried to tell her they were leaving (a groan of acknowledgement) followed by the room door opening, closing quietly and seeing John and Lorraine walking back to his apartment.

The next day, Lorraine called her. She was fine. Lorraine wondered if "we should simply have fucked her hard anyway, to get our money's worth." Not even they were that ruthless.

**

He sent her a black-and-white (often more sensual than the colour variety) of a woman lying on her side, with black bra and panties, her nipple emerging from one cup, her blindfolded, with her man lying behind her, with one hand plunged in the front of her panties, masturbating her, with the other round her neck.

I would love to re-enact this scene, you rubbing my pussy, tied and blindfolded. Yum! I am your slave in total submission. I have been a bad girl, please punish me! Take me! You own me! Take that pussy! I am tied up and you are fucking my tight ass! Yes, I deserve to be punished, by your hard huge cock up my puckering ass! I can barely speak, I am so horny!

I need to please you deep in my throat, John Evans!

***

That night, in bed, she presented her ass to him and he obliged. Those who are experienced in such things know that a certain delicacy is involved: that first penetration, passed the initial point of resistance, then slithering deep into her. In Lorraine's case, once that initial full insertion was complete and the gentle rhythm followed, she would push harder and harder against him, wanting him deeper and deeper. They knew when to stop.

She was begging for more attention and started to annoy him, to make him angry, on purpose, while alluding to that picture.

"I want to whip you because you're being an irritating bitch!" he said.

"Oh my god, do it you bastard!"

He leapt from the bed and was about to get the whip when he thought about putting on his gloves and smacking her around a bit.

"Where are you going?" Lorraine asked as he opened the wardrobe. He slipped his gloves on. "Why are your hands behind your back?

"Turn over!" he ordered.

She did and with her ass and back so presented, he started to smack her, hard then harder. All she did was moan and writhe with obvious delight and so much more.

"Turn over and open your legs, wide!"

She did. He stroked her cunt; more groans... then he smacked her there, again and again and again. She was loving it. He took her breasts and squeezed hard. He took her nipples and did the same. She was in heat.

He took out her requested purchase of wooden, sprung clothes pegs. He attached one to each nipple and looked closely at her expression; pleasure. He attached two more to the side of her breasts. He threw caution to the wind, wanted to emulate some porn pictures, separated her outer pussy lips and proceeded to attach ten – yes, ten – to each side. He checked on her again; nothing but gentle moans, the odd 'fuck' and an almost yoga-like serenity. His fevered reaction to her attempting to make him angry waned. He kissed her in acknowledgement of both her courage and her pleasure, removed each peg, gingerly, raised one of her legs, he now lying on his side (it was their relaxed fucking style), entered her, kissed her cheek, had his left hand propping his head up, took her left breast in his other hand and proceeded to fuck her (and indeed, her, him), until they stopped. He turned out the light, they moved into 'spoons' and fell asleep.

***

She was still in heat for more pussy; this was two weeks later, though nothing was planned. It was a holiday weekend. He had decided not to cook that Saturday night, instead treating her to a restaurant meal. They consumed a bottle of South Australian chardonnay: he was no wine connoisseur but this was particularly nice.

"Heather keeps calling and texting me," Lorraine said. "I haven't seen her for about six months. We drank a lot, I stripped her and sucked her pussy. She was hot! Will I contact her for us?"

John was genuinely ambivalent. He was finally persuaded. Two hours later, this young, well-proportioned with medium but perpendicular breasts came in. They drank some more – Lorraine's usual massive consumption capacity which disturbed both him and his pocket, considerably. Her fee was agreed, unbeknown to him at the time. They repaired to his apartment this time, a change of policy because she was a friend. Of course, this flew in the face of their mutual declaration but her almost agonised hunger for pussy circumvented any principle. Another bottle of wine was produced. It was consumed, then they were consumed; all three of them. The pattern was the same. They started on each other, to John's pleasure before they turned on his: he being manoeuvred into position by Lorraine, having affixed the required protection on to his erect manhood. He pumped her friend and she came. He restrained matters for himself, wanting to fuck his own woman. He did and they both took pleasure in Heather watching and obviously enjoying; she said so time and again.

Things calmed down and the girls, in order to subdue – or was it to recover – from their ardour, went into the bathroom and smoked some weed, acquired on the way back from the bar to his apartment. He let them chunter for a while. He then, being horny himself, decided to join them in the bathroom. There was a pall of weed-smoke. He didn't care. They were both naked, Lorraine standing against the sink, Heather sitting on the toilet. He lunged at Lorraine, turned her round and shoved his cock into her cunt. He started pumping. The girls were both semi-high, he stone-cold sober. He told Heather to stroke his ass and his balls. She did, with skill and dexterity. He found himself in the uncharacteristic situation of actually about to cum (as happened recently). He did, shooting himself deep into Lorraine's cunt. He almost whimpered with pleasure. As he withdrew, Lorraine fell to her knees and administered her conventional cleaning routine: sucking his cock, tasting his cum and sucking some more, until she was satiated and tired. All three acknowledged the particular joy of such a spontaneous episode, washed hands, brushed teeth, went to bed, cuddled in a triple sandwich, with John in the middle, talked a little and found themselves in almost the same position when they woke the following morning. John fucked Lorraine again – she wanted it – while Heather remained asleep. It was a delight.

35.

My happiness!
I am still on cloud nine. I don't know if I am dreaming or half awake! It's exhilarating, this new found joy! It's very scary because I want to hold on to it as tight as I can! You have the ability to calm and stir me very vigorously! (So many exclamations!) I am seeing you for the first time. I am appreciating you fully for the first time; your whole self, your amazing rock hard sexy body! Your amazing prowess with your huge tool; how you love me with passion. What are we going to do, John? Being with you gives me the greatest joy!

Mmmh, since we have booked a cottage and you did not object, meaning you have some thoughts of what could happen (tell me I am right!) and then, tell me what do you think could happen? Indulge me, sweets.

She was obviously enamoured by the various recent experiences. All had ended well. Then...

First, thank you for telling me and acknowledging your feelings of joy and more... It's rewarding to read as well as being a 'turn-on'! As for indulging you – 'what could happen'? It depends on many things including the atmosphere of the place, the genuine privacy and so on, but let's speculate just a little.

1. We shall have all our new toys.

2. I shall have the blindfold and ties.

3. If there is a verandah where no one can see, I might tie you up with your arms suspended, the blindfold on, and the whip being administered, all to the sound of the lapping sea.

4. If the bed is four-postered, you might be tethered to it, splayed apart, with the lights dimmed, our candle burning and the wax, drip, drip dripping on to your soft smooth skin, with pain...

5. The shower might be suitably inviting for some water sports, golden showers before I use such unspeakably bad language and describe such awful images, before you are bent over and your asshole is penetrated first with tongue then finger then rock hard cock!

6. ...and last for now, you might simply beg for something truly depraved to be done to you that I have never thought of, that you beg and beg for, that it is so awful, that I hesitate, before acceding to your pleading.

Enjoy the dreams and feel free to share your-slave-like possibilities. You *are* my slave and I *am* your master!

Good morning, Gorgeous! *Let me reply.*

1. We shall have all our new toys. *Yes we definitely will! Are we carrying the dildo?*

2. I shall have the blindfold and ties. *I would love that!*

3. If there is a verandah where no one can see, I might tie you up with your arms suspended, the blindfold on, and the whip being administered, all to the sound of the lapping sea. *We shall see but would not want to be found tied up.*

4. If the bed is four-postered, you might be tethered to it, splayed apart, with the lights dimmed, our candle burning and the wax, drip, drip dripping on to your soft smooth skin, with pain... *Mmmmhh, trembling with excitement and fear!*

5. The shower might be suitably inviting for some water... *Yes, when we come back to our room and are a bit tipsy... don't take it too seriously about being tipsy, it's the only time I am comfortable to let my other self out, and I enjoy it. It's part of it. Remove it and I don't think it will be as intense; .tipsy is part of the package.*

6. ...and last for now, you might simply beg for something truly depraved... *Mmmmh, you would have done so much to my poor tormented body, but I am sure that my erotic mind will come up with something.*

***

The weekend came and went in a flurry of activity.

First, thank you so much for allowing me to tie you up – more accurately, tying you down and letting hot wax be poured on to your breasts and your cunt.

Secondly, the weekend away was good but we still had tensions, which we both acknowledged and agreed to overcome in future.

Thirdly, on three separate occasions you declared that you "wanted to get married, have a family..." and you "will get out of Sierra Leone - I mean it!" On all three, I am of little use to you. The family business you know about. Getting out of Sierra Leone? My problem is that I am dependent on this country for work: at least till August 2015 and with luck, till August 2017. By then, the girls will have graduated (one year earlier) and the US house (for which I pay a large mortgage and tax bill) will, I hope, be sold, relieving me of the need for such a large income (by then, I doubt I will have full-time work anyway). Thus, when I say I don't have money, I mean it. It's not 'negative', it's the reality. Most of my income goes to the USA. For example, this weekend was a treat. It was either the trip or the swimming fee. Swimming has been ruled out for logistical reasons, so the decision was easy: weekend of pleasure with you!

Fourthly, you threatened some of the weekend by your assumptions: that I pay your taxi-fare for a journey I had nothing to do with; that you threaten discomfort or at least unpleasantness if I decline to buy you cigarettes in that club, through your semi-drunken stupor; when you searched for and picked up that girl; you declined to go to the dance floor with me but you did with her and frankly erotically so; I was the appendage, the convenience, the person with the money. I'm not your 'Sugar Daddy' and I object strongly to buying you cigarettes. I dislike your fundamental assumptions here. Even worse: you expect me to pay for your 'special smoking items' for which I do not participate either. It's simply wrong.

Finally and most fundamentally though, I need you to show some 'clear thinking'. This love of ours is incredibly skewed in my favour. It is you who has to do the sacrificing; the children thing and leaving Sierra Leone. Leaving Sierra Leone is possible but not in the short term for me. Children? No! I have four (one of whom will never grow up; because of that, he is already institutionalised for life). I therefore know that 'clear thinking is needed'. If I was ruthless, I would stop this now and let you fulfill these normal life-ambitions elsewhere but I'm not ruthless in this context. I want the selfish pleasure and joy of staying with you; keeping you to myself; possessing you. I get the benefits: older lusting man with gorgeous younger and erotic woman. You get your longed for 'darker side' partner (with love) but little else.

All I ask is that you think clearly about what you are giving up for me. I just don't want you, in a couple of years (when I am into my seventieth year, for heaven's sake!) to start resenting me for the obvious life-sacrifices you will have to make if you are to stay with me!

See you on Tuesday!

He just wanted to get things off his chest, assuming that she would see it as such and respond with a modicum of maturity. It was a plea for reality – which he wanted, in their pornographic ecstasy. He wanted her to realize the wider scheme of things.

What transpired stunned him; it shook him to his core. She sent him a 'rain-check' text about Tuesday, her next sleep-over date.

The 'rain-check' for the idea of returning on Tuesday, after his explanatory e-mail, had now lasted twenty-four hours. An e-mail then came through.

I have had time to think. For me, the only answer that keeps popping up is maybe, go back to no strings attached, no expectations... or not all. What do you think?

John replied:
I don't think that's possible. You could be with whoever you wanted and the same with me. Sorry, Lorraine. We tried. I failed. Why would I be with you, then be with someone else? Beats me!

Anyway, I was suggesting an NSA relationship with you, meaning expecting no future prospects or anything but if that's how you feel and see things, you are entitled. I tried my utmost best; clearly not enough. I give up. Good luck, John. I will surely miss you and us. Bye.

John responded, in utter disbelief: I'm so sorry to have failed you.

Last favour? Please get rid of my pictures. I can only hope... good luck!

He wrote: That is without question. It's a simple courtesy to you.

What flashed in his mind was to offer his sexual services to her for money and for her to return the same amount to him (thus, to be reciprocating whores, exclusively, without actually being 'out of pocket') because the sex – both normal and the dark side – was fantastic. In fact, he wondered if she might suggest such a thing; he considering her positive response to the idea to be at least a sixty-six per cent probability. Among other things, it was based on the premise of her willingness to sell him to selected others (mature and sophisticated – but frustrated – women, with her watching, supervising and administering the whole thing – a delicious thought in itself, all at her behest). He was tempted, sorely so, but this time he resisted. The negative stuff outweighed all. There was no alternative woman 'in the wings'; he would be alone again. He was resisting on a point of principle. Integrity had entered the scene – damn it!

36.

Within a week, they were trying yet again. She joined him at their breakfast brunch location. Neither was sure how either would react. It turned out to be a delight. They went back to her place and fucked like demented animals yet again. It was delicious.

The following two weeks, he was out of town, so only the weekends were available. The first was uneventful only in that she was introduced to his former director; the Swedish company he was with for two years before Sierra Leone. It was a small niche player, a good employer that paid on time. Frederick was worldly and took them both to a Lebanese restaurant within walking distance of the sports bar, where the men had earlier watched English Premier League football. Lorraine had the delight of walking in immensely high and patterned heels, over dug-up earth (new Wi-Fi cabling) and broken kerbs (rotten maintenance).

The meal was suitably Lebanese: delicious for them as John pawed his way through the assortment of non-British traditional fare. Lorraine showed her own sophistication in this regard.

***

Later, at her place, John administered one of her fantasies; to be tied up by the wrists, tethered to cupboard handles, well above her head. She was beaten with a whip; the erotic variety, bought on line through Amazon as part of an assortment of toys. She loved it. Her back, ass and thighs were attended to first. She wore one of his shirts; already ripped and therefore inviting more tearing. That was done. Each tear yielded more gasps of pleasure as the tails of the whip licked her gorgeous body.

He sensed tiredness and let her down, told her to lay on her back, now completely naked. More whipping, across her thighs, on to her breasts (something she really lusted after) and her pussy, with her legs now wide open, beckoning for more and more…

She was turned over, pulled on to her knees, was lubricated with baby oil and with remarkable ease, her asshole was penetrated; slowly, graciously and very, very deeply. Her pleasure was simply a beautifully depraved craving. Once finished, she masturbated. She came, frantically well. She recovered then started on him, setting him off with her manual dexterity before wanting him to take over. As he did, she teased his mind with the prospect of 'extra pussy' to be available 'to watch and to fuck'. She was determined to procure the same and to take it further, in a suitable Asian location and secure the delightfully wicked skills of a shemale; "you will suck her and then you'll fuck her as I take over the sucking of her cock." In this atmosphere, the orgasm was sensational.

***

The following weekend was one of Friday, a nice meal followed by more glorious sex. Saturday was touring other parts of town, to find good sports bars, getting them both out of the apartment, then disappointment as her two friends appeared and through peer pressure, she stayed with them and drank herself into a stupor. This had happened before, drinking and smoking to excess and topping it with a bit of weed.

He wasn't too well anyway, having caught his first head-cold in over six years – which, in his case, would inevitably get into his chest. The Sunday morning was an initial respite for her, with no headache." However, there was occasional vomiting; "this lasts for two days," she said; "don't worry.. She still found the energy to fuck and be fucked. One ambition, often expressed but never achieved was the golden shower; to piss and be pissed upon. All men know that pissing and an erection are mutually exclusive. On this Sunday morning, his manhood was languid.

He seized his opportunity and dragged her into the shower, sat her down and told her to open her mouth. She did and after an initial strain and trickle, the full flow poured. She took it all in her mouth and when full, spat it out and took more… It was an intoxicating experience, both to execute the deed and to see her consuming (before spitting some out). He kissed her mouth immediately after; "tastes like a very weak whisky." She agreed and started laughing.

***

Twenty-four hours later, he wrote to her.

When I left you yesterday, I heard voices but didn't recognise anything; I was concerned just with walking. You later told me that it was Alice and Kate in the vehicle. If I'd recognised, I would have acknowledged. I thought you couldn't tolerate Kate's company any more; wrong again on my side.

I walked and walked. Going uphill past the hospital. I couldn't breathe well. My chest felt very, very heavy. My thighs were not receiving oxygen; I slowed down. Once on the flat, after that uphill climb to Bintumani, the breathing system recovered. I have never felt like that since Ethiopia.

The mall was approached thirty-five minutes after leaving your place; 2.4 miles at my speed. I took a taxi the rest of the way.

About eight years ago, I was diagnosed as having COPD; you should look it up. It stands for chronic obstructive pulmonary disorder. It's supposed to be worse than asthma. I've always rejected the diagnosis, with Dar, and now Freetown, proving otherwise... until, that is, yesterday. Having a head cold triggers all such nonsense; the tight chest, the restricted exhalations and so on.

I am not supposed to smoke. I have never smoked. Secondary inhalation is almost as bad. I get that in your company a lot. You smoke to excess.

I don't drink much. You drink at least twice and even three-times as much as me. Saturday night was my first experience of your absence (from bed) because of friends (OK) and drink (not OK), witnessed by your hangover and vomiting the following day. You drink to excess.

Then your friends came again. When you called I could hear the cheerful chatter, laced with drink, I'm sure. If you weren't under the influence, you would have called again later, or sent a message by text or email. You did none of these. You really do drink to excess and it makes me feel uncomfortable.

In contrast: you dream of things on the dark side. You think to excess. I want this and more, very much indeed.

In the same way, you fuck to excess and more. I want this also, although you showed intolerance when I was a little tired (ill) and you suggested the honeymoon period was over. Selfish of you!

In short, that comment plus your smoking and your drinking is self-centered and self-destructive in the extreme. Your dark side dreams and fucking for more and more is wonderful in the extreme. No wonder I am having difficulties working out who the real you is?

This was, in essence (already), his last throw of the dice: to get her to wake up to certain realities so that the 'bad' excesses could be removed and the 'good' excesses nurtured and taken further. Here was the world of difference between writing about their dreamed realities and living them. The 'living' was proving to be immensely difficult.

She replied:

I do not know how to really respond to this.

First of all, I am truly sorry for exposing you to secondary smoke. It's a vice that I have been trying to cut down and eventually quit. It is a terrible habit that I do not like any more, It's ugly and now is causing trouble. I had made a vow to never smoke in your presence. I guess I got comfortable and ordered them. It's wrong and selfish of me. I agree on that one and want to promise you that I will never do it in your presence. For now, then, I will quit... I hope today!

Why did you walk? If you woke me up, I would have arranged a cab for you. I am truly sorry about the disorder. I would like to know more about it.

I do not live alone, John, and I did not mean for you to feel uncomfortable. Why would I do that? Selfish of me? I am in wonder.

I do not appreciate the insinuation that I am an alcoholic. I do not drink alcohol the whole week, only when we go out and the rare occasions, here at home when we have visitors. It's very true. You can do your research. I rarely have a drink on my own. Alice quit drinking. That day was the first time she has had alcohol. It's been easier not having a drink at home because of it. I can drink excessively, that I know but I have not been doing that for a long time save for Saturday and yesterday, which will put me off alcohol for some time.

I have never been accused of being selfish! Quite the contrary, actually! You have called me that on numerous times and it's hurtful. I try to show you how I care for you and you never seem to recognize it. I am starting to feel that you do not like Lorraine as a person but you love my dark fantasy and that's what's making you stay with me. I do not think I am okay with it. I am starting to suspect that you are not in love with me. You love the sex part. I am crying right now because this is the first time I am addressing what I have been feeling for some time.

I do not know what to do. I feel like we have gone back to a bad space, where we have been before. I am shaking with real fear that I am going to get hurt terribly and I will not know how to heal my heart again.

Maybe we should communicate through mail today if you will let us.

I have tried to show and tell you about me but sometimes you shush me (hurtful but okay) or stop my stories mid-sentence. What you see in me is what you get. I try not to be pretentious about anything especially with you. It seems like my efforts are lost on you. I just think you see so many wrongs in me and now I feel totally rotten.

What do you want, John? Be brutally honest with yourself and me. Are you in love or infatuated with my dark side? If it is the latter, I beg you let me know! I need to know! What can you not figure out about me anyway?

I am sorry for being such a bitch; rotten with excessive drinking and smoking.

I am sorry... xxx
PS; I just dumped all the cigarettes in the kitchen sink and ran the water over them.

He called her... jumped into a taxi, arrived, took her arm, sort of forcibly and pulled her into her bedroom. He peeled off her clothes, removed his own and fucked her hard, the way she liked it, again and again...

He got back home and resumed working, with his office bereft of the internet that day.

Thank you for love-fucking me back to happiness. It was the best surprise and oh so yummy! I will let you get on with your work while I start on mine.
You are the best!

'Much appreciated, Baby!' he replied. It was true, though. So was the explosive fucking.

37.

When things were stable, they agreed that he would see her on Friday evening, fuck and sleep over, fuck on Saturday morning, before leaving, shopping, going home to do his laundry then returning. They would fuck on Saturday night, then Sunday morning, before having their brunch in their chosen open-air restaurant; the full English breakfast including its master-stroke, black pudding He would sleep in his own place on Sunday and Monday night, partly for recovery, for letting his mind focus on his own stuff (writing mainly) and not rushing things. He'd be with her again on Tuesday, fucking and sleeping over, then reverting to his own world till Friday again.

This was now Tuesday again. He was so looking forward to it. He wrote to her:

Good morning, Beautiful! Just emerged from a meeting, Looking forward to your company and then your bed, tonight! Xxx

***

They had spoken more about the possibility of moving in together and choosing a new place. He even started surveying possible locations. Moving in together was an idea that erupted early, was treated cautiously by John but now, after this (what may have been their fifth attempt at reconciliation), it seemed a serious prospect. He must have been crazy. Did he love her? When it worked, 'yes'! Was he in love with her? He thought he was. He knew she was not a nice person in the sense of being homely but she was very, very exciting which appeared to carry each day.

He had stuff to do and agreed to be at her place by nine p.m. They spoke of her 'enterprise'; the design, manufacturing and marketing of high-class leather goods. He had encouraged her almost since they first met, four months earlier, to think about a business plan. He gave her a template. She completed part. They reviewed it. All was well. They went to bed.

Kissing and sucking: him on her (delicious) and her on him (phenomenal).

***

You've been with another woman. I can taste it! I can taste her!

He was stunned and in complete disbelief. For one thing, he'd never been with another woman since they met, except when she organised their threesomes; the first ending extremely badly, the next being inconclusive, the last ending completely calmly. This accusation was utter madness from her and he knew it. The trouble was, he didn't think she knew it; the sudden change in personality. On hearing that accusation, in the middle of some, frankly, searing foreplay, his own limited emotional intelligence kicked in.

His erection vanished. Not only had there been no other woman since they met but also, with her visual and sexual qualities and appetites, what need of other women?

"What on earth are you talking about?" he demanded.

"I think you live in two worlds; here and at your place and you fuck other women!"

He couldn't believe what she was saying.

"Why did you grab the phone from me so violently that time?"(She was referring to that awful time in his flat). "You could have broken my wrist!"

What she forgot to remember was that she was high, drunk, uncontrollable, had feigned, if not threatened, 'self-harm' with his bread knife – which he had wrenched from her grasp...

"You had no business wanting to check my phone for its contacts, messages or whatever," he told her. "I wouldn't do that to you!"

"You've been in contact with Heather!" Heather was the last successful threesome partner.

"What? How could I? I don't have any contact details; no phone, no email; nothing! Stop this. You're being ridiculous. This is crazy!"

The point was that the underlying suspicion – the fear of betrayal – that had triggered the drama in the night of their initially sumptuous but ultimately horrific threesome – was a subliminal impediment to a mature relationship. He was hoping that, in time, she would come to believe – with the idea of moving in together – that such genuine attempt at coming together would overcome all this stuff. The irony was that in contrast to his previous love, when he never 'felt safe', he actually felt completely safe with her and told her so, time and time again. This was ironic. Being the gorgeous looking creature that she was, she could have her pick of virile younger men but she chose John and, for some inexplicable reason, the possibility of her straying simply did not enter his mind.

Things quietened down, though he remained astonished at the accusation. Despite all this, he felt desire from her so his erection returned. He placed her on her back and invited enthusiasm which was duly granted. After a bit, he pushed her off because he simply wanted to pound her in the way she liked; deep, hard and rhythmic. He entered and as always, it felt like the first time; so tight, so beautifully gripping. He was slow, gentle then less so until he set into that piston-like fucking. He was propped up on his hands, looking at her, as he always did in that position. She was quiet. He spat on her face because she liked to be (mis-)treated as such.

"I'm not in the mood..." and with that all went limp and therefore quiet again. There was no fighting. This had never happened before. It wasn't the idea of being tired or unwell. There was dislike – contempt even – seeping from every pore in her body.

In previous times, he would have dressed, left and gone through the reconciliation ritual, sometime in the future. This time, he wanted to stay to see if wrongs could be righted.

He suggested that they watch a new TV series on her iPad; *Allegiance.* They did. He tired. She watched more and as she did, he could feel her disdain leeching from her body. He couldn't sleep. She left the bed, went to the sitting room and turned on the TV. Again, he tried to sleep but couldn't. It was now after two a.m. He joined her; him on the settee, her on the thick carpet beyond touching distance. About thirty minutes later, he lay on the settee. She came over and persuaded him to "come to bed". He did, with no ambition but sleep. He lay and felt her roll to her side; no contact. He had no yearning anyway; the original rejection and earlier accusation of 'another woman' – other women even – started to take hold. It was sickening.

At six fifteen a.m., the alarm went off. He realised she had been sleeping, tucked into his back; spoons. He offered no response in waking. He felt lousy emotionally and physically; the latter only because of the absence of that wonder of the human body – sleep. She offered coffee. He had no time as he fumbled with his clothes. A text confirmed that his taxi had arrived; it had been arranged the night before. He was to be taken home, to shower, have breakfast, change, walk the two miles to work (every day) and put in an intellectually rigorous day's work – all after about three hours sleep!

She saw him to the door. He made no attempt at endearment (despite the fact that she wore a tight-knit sweater skirt, with hoops that accentuated her delicate shape and frame). He looked at her as he walked out, climbed into the car and left. It was six thirty on Wednesday morning.

As he walked to the car, she said, "Please send me your other book!"

He thought this might be a return to her other, more normal self. He got home and obliged her.

That night an email came through. The torrent of accusations seemed to know no bounds.

You've just used me! You've done all this before! Do you use all women like this?

And so on and so forth....

When this basic theme had come from her before, he tried to explain that every previous encounter had been just that; an attempt to get to know a person who might be *the* person, the woman that encapsulated that notion of womanly *Perfection* according to his – apparently contorted – logic. All such previous encounters – attempts at a relationship – had failed. He thought, now, he had found her. The reconciliations seemed to suggest that. The recognition, through the torrid emails over the Christmas holiday period, even acknowledged that they needed to 'catch up emotionally'. He thought he was doing a reasonable job. He knew she'd been betrayed, apparently more than once. He was acutely aware of that and wanted to show her, over time, that if they could catch up emotionally, continue to enjoy each other's company and wallow in their erotic pleasures, things would come into balance and all would be well. The most recent accusation – "you've been with another woman" and the repeated refrain – "you've used me; I'm just another experiment" was evidence that things simply would not progress. Her fears were so deep-seated in her mind and frighteningly embedded in her heart, that the month of holiday messages were just wishful dreams. The reality, sadly, transpired differently.

***

At 1.05 p.m. the next day, a text came through:
I wish you all the best in all your endeavours. Cheers.

He was working intensely that day (the usual case) but took time to write a first draft response. He returned to it occasionally, fine tuning, getting the nuance as right as he could. At five thirty p.m., he sent his reply.

My dear Lorraine,

Your gentle 'sign-off' prompts me to write a day earlier than intended.

1. We both tried, again and again. It was a brave and genuine attempt. It's such a pity yet Tuesday was the realisation. My expression on Wednesday morning's departure was one of simple 'regret and resignation'.

2. My thoughts of you remain overwhelmingly positive... and please forgive my temporary lapse from sober language. You are by far and away the most terrific fuck I have ever experienced. The expressions of mutual love were powerful and genuine. The dark side was exciting in the extreme; things I have written of but never experienced. You brought that side to life! The sadness is that, for example, I finally managed to open that last link you sent and watched (what turned out to be) the shemale threesome – male, female and mixed, I then realised that the central pleasure in watching such stuff is to know that it is being shared with a gorgeous creature of 'like-mind'. That appears to be no longer the case.

3. As for me: I have already reverted to my existence of 'work, eat and sleep'. There is 'nobody in the wings'.

Please take care of yourself and try to make progress with your 'enterprise'.

P.S. Please don't dare return the gifts (clothes) bought. In time, they will simply prompt pleasant memories as you display your beauty (inner and outer).

At seven p.m., he checked his mail and found her reply.

Dear John,

My text was from a space of utter frustration and sadness and a sudden realisation of how you feel about me. It was not the drinking or the cigarettes. It was almost everything but the sexual side, I am truly saddened and upset, I feel played and cheated and used but that is okay. Again, I have jumped these horrible kinds of hurdles before and I will do it again.

These were games for you and it's very unfortunate.

I want you to have your 'gifts' back, I cannot keep them if I want to move on.

I had just thrown your other 'ties' away this morning, I will put them with your other stuff.

I WISH I NEVER MET YOU!

I hope you get your perfect woman.

I will never contact you again.

Bye.

Her reply was intensely sad for John because none of her assertions were true (but again, it had been an early and recurring theme in her argument).

For example: 'Reading your books, I feel manipulated!'

Another message came.

Should Fred (our trusted taxi driver) call you or leave the 'gifts' at the gate? They will be packed in a way no one will be able to see what's inside.

If you insist on doing this, have them left at the gate (for Apt 101).

If it's any consolation, I returned all the things my previous love bought, except those that I would have bought anyway.

I really don't give a shit about the toys – bin them please – but the clothes, please consider keeping them...

There was almost vitriol in her reply.

I will be packing everything. I want to forget that I ever knew you. I would never wear the clothes without remembering you, so calling Fred in a bit.

Don't you worry, I am staying away from Craigslist; it's the cause of all this stupid heartache. What did I expect anyway?

Cheers and have a good life.

Craigslist is how they met. 'What did (she) expect anyway?' That's easy!

'I am a lady in my early thirties, sexy witty and adventurous, slim and tall.
I am in search of a Caucasian man in his forties or early fifties, who is not looking for a LTR but for a lady friend to enjoy fantasy trials with. Write to me; a (no-nude) photo would be appreciated.'
It seemed too good to be true...

The End.